THE **FORTUNES** OF **TEXAS**

SHIPMENT 5

Mendoza's Secret Fortune by Marie Ferrarella
The Taming of Delaney Fortune by Michelle Major
My Fair Fortune by Nancy Robards Thompson
Fortune's June Bride by Allison Leigh
Plain Jane and the Playboy by Marie Ferrarella
Valentine's Fortune by Allison Leigh

SHIPMENT 6

Triple Trouble by Lois Faye Dyer
Fortune's Woman by RaeAnne Thayne
A Fortune Wedding by Kristin Hardy
Her Good Fortune by Marie Ferrarella
A Tycoon in Texas by Crystal Green
In a Texas Minute by Stella Bagwell

SHIPMENT 7

Cowboy at Midnight by Ann Major
A Baby Changes Everything by Marie Ferrarella
In the Arms of the Law by Peggy Moreland
Lone Star Rancher by Laurie Paige
The Good Doctor by Karen Rose Smith
The Debutante by Elizabeth Bevarly

SHIPMENT 8

Keeping Her Safe by Myrna Mackenzie
The Law of Attraction by Kristi Gold
Once a Rebel by Sheri WhiteFeather
Military Man by Marie Ferrarella
Fortune's Legacy by Maureen Child
The Reckoning by Christie Ridgway

THE **FORTUNES** OF **TEXAS**

A SWEETHEART FOR JUDE FORTUNE

———————— ✗ ————————

Cindy Kirk

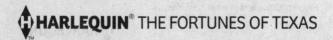
HARLEQUIN® THE FORTUNES OF TEXAS

Special thanks and acknowledgment are
given to Cindy Kirk for her contribution to The
Fortunes of Texas: Welcome to Horseback Hollow continuity.

ISBN-13: 978-1-335-68052-5

A Sweetheart for Jude Fortune

Recycling programs
for this product may
not exist in your area.

Printed in U.S.A.

www.Harlequin.com

From the time she was a little girl, **Cindy Kirk** thought everyone made up different endings to books, movies and television shows. Instead of counting sheep at night, she made up stories. She's now had over forty novels published. She enjoys writing emotionally satisfying stories with a little faith and humor tossed in. She encourages readers to connect with her on Facebook and Twitter, @cindykirkauthor, and via her website, cindykirk.com.

To my longtime friend, author
Nancy Robards Thompson.
Here's to many, many more years of friendship!

Chapter 1

Standing on the sidewalk outside the Horseback Hollow Superette on a bright Friday morning, Gabriella Mendoza paused to read a text from her father, sent from his room in a rehabilitation center in Lubbock.

Bath@9. DON'T come b4 10.

Gabi sighed. Since it was barely eight-thirty, even if she chugged down the highway at the speed of a slug, she'd easily make the one-hour drive into the city before ten. This meant she needed to use this stop at the local convenience store to not only grab coffee, but kill time.

OK C U after 10, she texted back, then started

toward the store known for carrying a little bit of everything. She was mentally calculating how much time she needed to waste when her phone pinged.

Gabi smiled. Though Orlando Mendoza had recently celebrated his sixtieth birthday, he texted with a fervor normally reserved for teenagers. She'd barely glanced at the incoming message when her forward progress came to a jarring halt.

"Whoa." The masculine voice held a hint of laughter. Large hands reached out to steady her when she stumbled.

Startled, Gabi jerked her head up and the unsteadiness returned full force. Even if his eyes hadn't been the color of the Texas sky, the blond-haired Adonis in worn Wranglers and a black Stetson would have caused any red-blooded woman's heart to race.

"Whoa," Gabi repeated.

He lifted his hands from her forearms, but the searing heat from his touch lingered. "Are you okay? I plowed right into you."

"Actually, I think it was me plowing into you." She flashed a quick, apologetic smile. "I'm one of the rare few who can't walk and read a text at the same time."

"Let's call it a draw." The cowboy offered up a lazy smile and rocked back on his heels. He made no move to step aside or walk away. It was as if he had all the time in the world to stand in the bright sunlight of this unseasonably warm day in late January and chat with a stranger.

And Gabi *was* a stranger, not only to him but to most of the two thousand residents living in this small North Texas town. Though she'd been living in her father's house in Horseback Hollow for the past couple weeks, she had yet to meet his neighbors. Since she'd arrived from her home in Miami, any free time had been spent at the hospital.

When she'd been notified the small plane her father had been flying had crashed, Gabi had hopped the first flight to Texas. With her mother dead and her brothers unable to make the trip for various reasons, she'd come alone.

Gabi hadn't minded the sacrifice. Her father had always been there for her. All she wanted was him to be independent once again. His transfer from the hospital to rehab yesterday had been a positive first step.

Hopefully with her father doing better, she'd have the opportunity to meet a few people in town. Like now, she could spend a few minutes flirting—er, becoming acquainted with—the handsome hunk who stood before her, without feeling she was neglecting her dad.

Unfortunately, before Gabi could formulate

something smart and witty to say, his phone rang. The cowboy glanced at the screen, grimaced and answered.

"Have a fabulous day," she said softly, regretfully, wiggling her fingers goodbye.

He shot her a wink. Even as he listened intently, phone pressed to his ear, those clear blue eyes remained fixed on her. The scrutiny made her glad she'd taken a few extra minutes this morning to dab on some makeup and curl her hair instead of pulling it back like she'd been doing all week.

As Gabi entered the Superette, she almost called back that it had been nice to meet him. She stopped herself just in time.

They hadn't met, not really. They'd merely run into each other—literally—and exchanged a handful of words. She didn't even know his name. Of course, that didn't mean she hadn't liked what she'd seen, and it certainly didn't stop her from hoping he'd be there when she came out.

But, by the time she returned with a twenty-ounce cup of decaf in hand, he was gone. Heaving a sigh of regret, Gabi slid behind the wheel of her father's boat-of-a-Buick and turned toward the highway leading to Lubbock.

The car obediently settled into a smooth cruise, allowing her brain to shift to autopilot.

She'd made this trip to see her father more times in the past few weeks than she could count.

When the landing gear on the plane he'd been flying had failed to engage, the experienced aviator had been forced to belly-land. Most of his injuries had been incurred when the plane broke apart on impact. She'd seen pictures of what was left of the Cessna.

What had the doctor said? *It was a miracle he'd survived.*

Gabi rolled up the window all the way, suddenly chilled to the bone. But she reminded herself that was the past. Today was her father's first full day in the rehabilitation center and a cause for celebration.

By the time Gabi pulled into the parking lot of the facility, her mood was as sunny as the cloudless sky. She headed toward the front door of the facility with a bounce in her step.

Once inside, she quickly located the stairs. Seizing opportunities to exercise came so naturally Gabi never considered taking an elevator. She jogged up the steps two at a time, pleased her heart rate remained steady and her breath even.

Six years ago she hadn't been able to make it across even the smallest room without needing to sit down. Now her heart beat strong in a body as toned as an athlete's.

The walls lining the hallway leading toward her father's room were filled with pictures and inspiring stories of rehab center "alumni." With splashes of bright colors throughout and rooms with state-of-the-art equipment discreetly out of sight, the facility had a cheerful feel.

Doing her best to ignore the faint medicinal scent hanging in the air, Gabi stopped in front of room 325 and gently rapped her knuckles against the closed door.

"Come in," she heard her father say.

She paused. Did he realize it was her and not a nurse or therapist? Pushing the door open only a couple of inches, she paused. "It's Gabriella. Are you decent?"

Orlando Mendoza's deep, robust laugh was all the answer she needed. She pushed open the door and stepped inside.

Her father sat in a chair by the window, wearing a blue shirt with thin silver stripes and the navy pants she'd altered a couple days ago to accommodate his left leg cast. While the past few weeks had added extra streaks of silver to his salt-and-pepper hair, Orlando Mendoza remained a strikingly handsome man.

He lifted his right hand in greeting, drawing her attention to the cast that encased the arm. Seeing it brought back memories of the day in the intensive care waiting room when the doctor had sat down with her and detailed the injuries: fractured left leg and right arm, bruised kidneys, fractured rib, concussion.

But her father was tough. And determined. Perhaps it was the sight of him dressed in street clothes or the bright smile of greeting on his lips, but for the first time since the accident, Gabi truly believed he'd make it all the way back.

"Papi." She crossed the room, placing her coffee cup on a tray table before leaning down and wrapping her arms around him. "You look like yourself."

"As opposed to looking like someone else?" he asked with a teasing smile.

She laughed and pushed back to hold him at arm's length. If not for the arm and leg cast, Gabi could believe her father was simply enjoying a cup of coffee before heading to the Redmond Flight School where he worked. As a retired former air force pilot, flying had been his life for too many years to count.

When he'd gotten the opportunity two months ago to help run a flight school in Texas, he'd been as excited as a graduate landing his first job. While Gabi had been sad to see him leave Florida, she'd also been happy for him. The position was exactly what he'd been looking for since he'd retired from the air force.

And since the crime rate in the area of Miami

where he lived had skyrocketed in recent years, she'd found comfort in the knowledge he was now in a small rural community.

"What are you thinking, *mija?*" her father probed, his tone gentle.

Gabi expelled a heavy sigh. "I thought you'd be safe in Horseback Hollow."

"He should have been."

Gabi turned toward the masculine voice to see her father's two bosses standing in the doorway. Sawyer Fortune had met her at the airport when she'd flown in from Miami after getting news of the accident. His new wife, Laurel, had remained by her father's side at the hospital.

In the difficult days that followed, they'd been her rock.

"Are you feeling up to company?" Laurel asked Orlando. She was a tall, pretty blonde with long hair pulled back in a ponytail. "If not, Sawyer and I can stop back later."

"You're not company." Orlando motioned them into the room and gestured to the small sitting area near his bed. "Please, sit."

After exchanging greetings and hugs, Gabi also took a seat and let her father direct the conversation. She could tell it made him feel good to have Sawyer and Laurel stop by on a workday to see him.

She sipped her coffee, offering a word now

and then when appropriate. When the talk turned to sabotage, Gabi straightened in her seat. She fixed her gaze on Sawyer. "Are you saying someone deliberately messed with the landing gear?"

Sawyer raked a hand through his brown hair. Though it wasn't even noon, weariness clouded his eyes. He expelled a harsh breath. "We don't know for sure, not yet."

"Who would do such a thing?" Gabi's voice rose and broke. An accident was one thing, but for someone to deliberately set out to hurt her father... "He just moved here. He doesn't have enemies."

Laurel and Sawyer exchanged a glance.

Gabi's breath hitched. "Does he?"

"We don't think it's about him," Sawyer said finally. "The sheriff thinks someone may be out to get the Fortunes."

"*Your* family?" Gabi struggled to recall what she'd heard about the Fortunes. *Wealthy* and *prominent* were the only words that came to mind. "Why?"

"*Mija.*" The endearment slid off Orlando's lips as he reached over with his left hand and captured her fingers, giving them a squeeze. "The authorities are still investigating. All this is simply speculation."

The older man cast a sharp look in Sawyer's

direction as if telling him there would be no more upsetting talk in front of his daughter.

Yet, it was Laurel, not Sawyer, who changed the subject. She shifted her attention to Gabi. "Now that you've had some time to settle in, what do you think of Horseback Hollow?"

"It's a nice town." Out of the corner of her eye Gabi saw her father nod approval. Even if she hadn't liked it here, she wouldn't have said otherwise. But she'd spoken the truth. Though she'd never considered herself a small-town girl, so far she was enjoying her stay. "I find it very peaceful."

Laurel smiled encouragingly. "Tell me what you've been doing to keep yourself busy."

"Well, I spend most of my days with Papi." Gabi slanted a glance and he smiled. "Since the weather has been unseasonably warm, I try to go for a run once I leave the hospital."

"To *try* isn't good enough. You mustn't neglect your exercise." Her father's voice brooked no argument. "It's essential."

Gabi bit back a sharp reply that would have been worthy of a brash fifteen-year-old rather than a mature woman of twenty-six. Instead she smiled. "I've gone for a run every day except the day I flew in."

"I always feel better when I exercise, too," Laurel agreed, a look of understanding in her eyes. "But I hope while you're here, you also take time to get acquainted with the people and the town."

The image of the man at the Superette flashed before Gabi. Yes, getting to know the cowboy would be a pleasure.

"I've gotten acquainted with you and your husband," Gabi said when she realized Laurel waited for an answer. "Now, when I return to Miami and Papi talks of Sawyer and Laurel, I'll know just who he means."

Sawyer inclined his head. "Are you planning on going back soon?"

"Not until my father is home and able to care for himself."

"You have a job," Orlando protested. "I won't put your position in jeopardy. Even the most understanding employer can lose patience when days turn into weeks."

"I took family medical leave," Gabi told her father for what felt like the zillionth time. "Staying isn't a problem."

"My daughter is a manager at Miami Trust." Pride filled Orlando's voice. "It's one of the largest banks in Florida."

"My boss was supportive of me coming." Gabi kept her tone soft and soothing. "You don't have to be concerned."

"I can't help but worry." Orlando lifted a shoulder in a shrug. "That's how I am."

It was true. Gabi remembered the lines that had seemed permanently etched between her father's brows when she'd gotten sick and needed surgery. Her mother's worry hadn't been as obvious, but Gabi knew they'd both spent many sleepless nights fearing for her life.

Impulsively Gabi leaned over and hugged her father. "That concern is one of the things I love about you."

Surprise flickered in his eyes. They'd had some battles in the past over what she'd termed his overprotectiveness, but once he'd moved to Texas, she discovered she rather missed having someone around who cared enough to worry.

Sawyer's phone trilled. He glanced down then rose to his feet with a look of regret. "I need to go."

"I appreciate you stopping by." Orlando's gaze shifted from Sawyer to Laurel. "Both of you."

"We want you back at the flight school." Laurel placed a hand on Orlando's shoulder, then bent and kissed his cheek. "It's not the same without you, O."

"Thanks for that." Orlando's cheeks turned a dusky pink before his tone turned brusque. "I'd walk you to the door but it took two nurses just to get me in the chair this morning."

Sawyer crossed the room to stand beside his employee. His eyes met the older man's dark brown eyes. "I promise you, if the plane *was* sabotaged, we'll get whoever was behind it."

"Thank you."

"Don't worry about your job," Sawyer told him. "It'll be there waiting for you. No matter how long you're off."

For a second, Gabi thought she saw the sheen of tears in her father's eyes, but when she looked again they were gone. She decided it must have simply been her imagination.

"I appreciate it" was all her father said.

Sawyer shifted those striking blue eyes in Gabi's direction. "I realize it's short notice but we're having a barbecue at the ranch tonight and—"

"We'd love to have you join us," his wife added with a bright smile. "I know you wanted to stay close while your father was in the hospital. Since he's now doing so well, I hope you'll consider coming this evening."

"Go," her father urged before Gabi could respond. "I'm planning on watching the ball game tonight."

"Sawyer's aunt and uncle as well as most of his cousins will be there." Laurel's tone turned persuasive. "They've lived in Horseback Hollow all their lives so if there's anything you want to know about the town or the area, they're the ones to ask."

Gabi couldn't imagine having too many questions about a town that was barely two blocks long.

"I can guarantee good food," Sawyer said when Gabi hesitated. "My aunt makes the best desserts, and she's promised to bring a couple of her specialties tonight."

"My Gabriella doesn't eat sweets." Orlando spoke before Gabi could respond. "It's not good for her. She—"

Gabi shot him a warning glance, and whatever else he'd been about to say died on his lips. Had she really missed his constant worry?

"Like everyone," Gabi said easily, "my goal is to eat healthy. That's not to say I don't enjoy a bite or two of something sweet occasionally."

Her father opened his mouth then shut it when she fixed her gaze on him.

"Please say you'll come." Laurel's eyes sparkled in her pretty face. "If only for a bite or two of Jeanne Marie's spectacular desserts."

Gabi considered. An honest-to-goodness Texas barbecue could be fun. God knew she was tired of hospital food. But this was her father's first night in rehab. How could she enjoy herself knowing he'd be sitting alone in his room watching a ball game by himself?

"There'll be lots of handsome men there."
Laurel shot her a little wink.

*As handsome as the man outside the coffee
shop?* Gabi wanted to ask. His eyes had been
as blue as Sawyer's and, like her father's boss,
the cowboy had a casual confidence she found
appealing.

"Tonight at seven, O?" a man in a wheelchair
called from the doorway.

"I'll meet you in the lounge," her father called
back.

Gabi lifted a brow.

"The ball game," Orlando informed her.
"Lloyd and I made plans to watch it together
when we were sweating to the oldies in physical therapy this morning."

Gabi turned to find Laurel staring at her with
an arched brow.

"Tell me when and where," Gabi told her. "I'll
be there."

Chapter 2

As she turned off onto the lane leading to Sawyer and Laurel Fortune's ranch, excitement quivered in Gabi's belly. Her first Texas barbecue at a real ranch. She glanced down at her skirt and sweater, hoping she wouldn't find herself over- or underdressed.

Before Laurel left the rehabilitation center today, she'd assured her the barbecue would be casual. But Gabi had painfully discovered on several occasions that *casual* meant different things to different people.

Since her Florida attire was too lightweight for even a warmer-than-normal North Texas winter, she'd stopped in nearby Vicker's Corners on the way back from Lubbock. The small town, just down the road from Horseback Hollow, had a cute little downtown area filled with quaint shops. At a darling boutique that rivaled those in Miami for selection and price, Gabi picked up the skirt, sweater, tights and boots she wore tonight.

The shawl collar of her cherry-red sweater showed very little skin, which meant there was no possibility of her scar showing. She felt like a coward for caring what people thought, but since the horrible pool party incident several months back, she now kept it fully covered.

Gabi drove slowly down the gravel lane flanked by white fence and miles of pasture-land. The fact that she hadn't yet spotted a single cow didn't surprise her. Sawyer had mentioned their ranch was basically a lot of land with a few horses. Laurel had laughingly added that bovines weren't their thing.

She wheeled the Buick between two dusty pickups and sat in the car for several seconds. Through one of the brightly lit windows, she caught a glimpse of Laurel, chatting with a guest, a glass of wine in her hand.

She liked Laurel. Liked her a lot. And Sawyer, as well.

Seeing how much her father mattered to them warmed her heart. Even knowing they shared Papi's passion for flying was a comfort.

After stepping from the large blue car, Gabi cinched the belt of the coat she'd picked up on her shopping trip today tightly around her. She wasn't sure what she was going to do with the pretty tweed once she returned home, but for tonight, with the wind holding a sharp bite, she was glad she had it.

Experiencing a sudden longing for palm trees and eighty-degree weather, Gabi sprinted to the porch and up the steps. She hunched her shoulders against the wind and punched the doorbell. She immediately shoved her hands into her pockets, regretting she hadn't thought to pick up a pair of gloves on her impromptu shopping trip.

Thankfully, the door opened before the chimes made it through a single stanza. Laurel stood in the doorway with her husband at her side, broad welcoming smiles on their lips. Gabi breathed a sigh of relief when she saw Sawyer wore jeans and a chambray shirt. Laurel's skirt and sweater mirrored Gabi's own attire.

"Come in," Sawyer urged, ushering her into the warmth. "It's freezing out there."

"I'm glad you made it." Her hostess took both of Gabi's hands and gave them a squeeze.

"Considering the weather, I wasn't sure you'd go through with the barbecue." Gabi resisted the urge to shiver. "I swear the temperature dropped twenty degrees in the past hour."

"We were forced to make a few adjustments." Laurel waited while Gabi handed her coat to a young woman dressed in black pants, white shirt and fire-engine-red cowboy boots. Then she looped her arm through Gabi's and ushered her farther into the house. "The barbecue is now indoors, centered around a crackling fire."

Happy to hear she wouldn't have to brave the wind and cold, Gabi took a moment to survey the interior of the large—and comfortably warm—house as they walked.

"You have a beautiful home." Gabi admired the open-beamed ceilings and dark shiny wood floors. Found the gilt Regency mirror above a Chippendale sideboard backed by timbered walls to be an appealing contrast.

"Thank you." Sawyer slipped an arm around his wife's waist. "We haven't lived here all that long, but it feels like home."

The words had barely left his lips when door chimes sounded. Laurel turned, but Sawyer gave her hand a squeeze. "Take care of Gabi. Introduce her around. I'll get the door."

"Don't worry about me—" Gabi began.

"It's my pleasure." Laurel sounded sincere. "We want you to have a good time this evening. You and your father are special to us."

Gabi let her gaze linger on the pretty, self-assured woman who'd been such a good friend to Papi. "I appreciate all you've done for him."

"Orlando is a great guy," Sawyer said, returning from the door.

"He's part of our family now," Laurel added.

"The Fortunes are a big family," Sawyer said. "But there's always room for one more good man."

Gabi blinked back unexpected tears. This connection was what she hoped her father would find when he'd moved so far from family. She swallowed against the lump in her throat and glanced around the room. "Are there a lot of Fortunes here?"

"My aunt and uncle and their children—my cousins—are with us this evening," Sawyer responded, before he turned to respond to a young boy's tug on his sleeve.

A big family. Children. Gabi had once thought that would be part of her future. Until the doctor had sat her down and laid out the risks....

"Most of the guests are back here." Laurel led her to the edge of a great room.

The line of windows flanking the back of the home gave an open, airy feel to a room that was even more spacious than the one they'd passed. A buffet table topped with a red-and-white-checkered cloth along one wall drew her eye.

Mason jars tied with red bandannas sporting yellow daisies were strategically placed between platters of barbecue pork, smoked ham and Texas beef brisket. From where she stood, Gabi could see bowls of baked beans, black-eyed peas and Brunswick stew.

On the hearth of a massive stone fireplace, galvanized washtubs filled with ice, bottles of beer and cans of soda beckoned.

At the moment Gabi couldn't decide if she was more interested in eating, drinking or socializing. The food looked terrific, but the laughter and chatter filling the air called to her. As she swept the room with her gaze Gabi noted all ages were represented from a baby held in the arms of a pretty young woman with long, tousled blond hair to a man and woman who appeared to be in their sixties. She wondered if they were Sawyer's aunt and uncle.

Despite considering herself a fairly social creature, Gabi liked having Laurel at her side. The sight of so many loud and boisterous individuals in one room was a bit overwhelming.

A burst of laughter sounded by a bar set up in an alcove had Gabi turning toward the sound. Her breath caught in her throat.

It was him. Her handsome cowboy from the Superette.

He might be standing with his back partially to her, but she'd recognize the disheveled dark blond hair and muscular build anywhere. Even dressed simply in jeans and a long-sleeved Henley, he looked every bit as yummy as he had that morning.

As her gaze lingered, the air began to sizzle. As if slapped alongside the head by a ball of charged molecules, the cowboy broke off what he was saying and shifted his stance.

When his eyes met hers, everything in Gabi went weak. She barely heard what Laurel said. Something about introducing her around?

With great effort she pulled her attention away from those mesmerizing eyes. "I'd like that."

Would Laurel introduce her to *him?* If not, from the gleam of interest she'd seen in his eyes, she knew her mystery man would make sure their paths crossed this evening.

Their first stop was in front of an attractive older woman with pale blue eyes and long silver hair fastened in a low bun. Her turquoise jewelry accentuated the Southwestern flavor of the simple flowing dress she wore. Despite the fact she wore flats and Gabi's boots had three-inch heels, the woman was still several inches taller than her five-two.

The look in her eyes was kind, her smile warm, and Gabi liked her instantly.

"This is Sawyer's aunt, Jeanne Marie Fortune

Jones," Laurel was saying, "and her husband, Deke."

Gabi widened her smile to include the rugged man with a thatch of thick gray hair.

As Laurel introduced her to the older couple, mentioning her connection to Orlando, the woman took her hand and pulled Gabi close.

"I'm so sorry about your father." Jeanne Marie's low soothing voice was a thick balm on Gabi's tattered spirit.

The solace she'd found in the woman's arms made Gabi realize just how much she missed her mother. Like Jeanne Marie, Luz Mendoza had been a demonstrative, affectionate woman who dispensed hugs freely and often.

"It's not right."

Gabi turned to Deke, surprised at the anger in his voice.

His eyes flashed. "Sabotage doesn't happen in this community."

"They don't know if it was sabotage. My father says the NTSB is still investigating." Gabi repeated what Orlando had told her. "It may have just been an unfortunate accident."

"More likely someone who doesn't like the Fortunes," Deke said loudly.

"Now you just hush." Jeanne Marie put a hand on her husband's arm. Her tone might be light but her eyes were steady and firm.

"Laurel mentioned your children are here tonight." Gabi spoke, eager to change the subject and ease the sudden tension in the air. "How many do you have?"

"Seven." A pretty young woman with a spray of freckles across her nose and tousled blond hair, who Gabi had noticed earlier, strolled up and answered for Jeanne Marie, then extended her hand.

"I'm number six, aka Stacey Fortune Jones." She gestured to the young woman next to her, so similar in appearance Gabi knew they must be sisters. "This is Delaney, the baby of the family."

Gabi introduced herself as Laurel stepped away to consult with the caterers and Jeanne Marie and Deke were pulled away by another couple.

"Stacey." Gabi tilted her head. "Are you by any chance the Stacey who administered first aid to my father after his accident?"

The woman nodded. "I stayed with him, did what I could until the rescue squad arrived."

Her father had called the nurse an angel sent from above. Gabi grasped Stacey's hands and emotion surged, clogging her throat. "From the bottom of my heart, thank you. We lost my mother a couple years ago. I—I don't know what I'd have done if I'd lost him, too."

Gabi's voice broke. She paused, took a steadying breath.

Stacey's eyes, as blue as her mother's, filled with understanding. "I was happy to help."

"Since my mother died it's just been me and my dad. My brothers aren't around much."

"Brothers?" Light danced in Delaney's pretty eyes. She stepped forward like a hound catching a scent. "How many do you have?"

"Four." Gabi counted them off on her fingers. "Matteo, Cisco, Alejandro and Joaquin."

"Older? Younger?" Delaney pressed.

"All older."

"We've got you beat." Delaney glanced at her sister. "We have *five* older brothers. Then our parents' luck changed."

"I broke the curse," Stacey said modestly.

"I arrived a year after Stace." Delaney flashed a smile. "They saved the best for last."

Gabi chuckled. "I always wanted a sister. Brothers can be nice but—"

"They can be a real pain," Stacey and Delaney said at the same time then laughed.

"Mine used to do all sorts of horrible things." Gabi shuddered, remembering. "Matteo once dropped a frog down my shirt. And Joaquin put a snake in my bed."

"If you think that's bad—" Delaney went on to share some of the trials she'd endured at her brothers' hands with Stacey chiming in with another long-ago incident her sister had forgotten.

"The strange thing is, now that they're grown and gone, I miss them," Gabi said, feeling a bit melancholy.

"We don't have a chance to miss ours." Delaney expelled a long sigh. "They're all still around."

Across the room a baby's voice shrieked with the gurgling laughter of the very young.

Gabi pulled her brows together and fixed her gaze on Stacey. "Didn't I see you holding a baby earlier?"

Stacey smiled. "That's my little girl, Piper. Colton has her now."

"Her fiancé." Delaney emphasized the word, gesturing to where a slim man with brown eyes and brown hair stood, holding the baby and talking to Gabi's mystery man. "Isn't he handsome?"

Gabi pulled her gaze from the cowboy she'd begun to think of as hers to Stacey's fiancé. "He is a cutie."

"I think so." The older sister's red lips curved. "But then, I'm partial."

"Colton isn't just good-looking, he's super nice." Delaney shot her sister a warm smile of approval.

"Who's he speaking with?" Gabi asked in what she hoped was a casual tone.

"That's Jude." Delaney rolled her eyes. "One of our crosses to bear."

Gabi inclined her head.

"A brother," Stacey clarified. "Number three of our seven. I'll introduce you."

Before Gabi could respond, Stacey called out, "Colton. Jude. Over here."

The two men turned together. Gabi swore she saw a light flare in Jude's eyes. *Jude.* She rolled the name around on her tongue, liking the feel of it.

He crossed the room with a rolling, confident gait and a lazy smile on his lips.

"Hey, pretty lady," Jude said immediately upon reaching her side. "Can a cowboy buy you a drink?"

Delaney and Stacey looked at each other and burst into laughter.

"With lines like that, no wonder you're not dating anyone," Stacey teased.

Delaney made a gagging noise, worthy of any younger sister.

Jude ignored them both, keeping his eyes firmly focused on Gabi.

"I wouldn't mind a ginger ale," she told him.

"Be right back," he said with a wink.

"He's got you in his crosshairs." Delaney spoke in a theatrical whisper.

"Run," Stacey urged, her eyes dancing, "while you still have a chance."

Colton shook his head. "Women."

"Hey!" Stacey gave her fiancé a playful punch. "You've got two women in your life now, remember. Me and Piper?"

He brushed his lips across her cheek. "And I'm extremely glad of it."

Jude returned with a beer in one hand for himself and a ginger ale in the other for Gabi.

"Thank you." Gabi took the glass, her hand brushing his. Electricity traveled up her arm at the contact. But if he'd experienced a similar jolt, it didn't show.

Once again, Gabi suffered through introductions and expressions of sympathy for her father.

"I wouldn't have left him in the rehab center alone," Gabi explained, "but he's watching the ball game with another patient."

"I bet it makes him feel good to know you're out enjoying yourself." Colton looped an arm around his fiancée's shoulder when she moved to his side.

"I hope so," Gabi said, then made a fuss over Piper, rather than focusing on Jude, which is what she wanted to do. Though she was definitely in the mood for a little fun flirting, there was no need to be obvious.

She'd barely lifted Piper from Colton's arms

when several more handsome cowboys stopped over. None of them made her pulse skip a beat like number three of seven but Galen, Liam, Toby and Christopher Fortune Jones were all fine specimens.

When Piper began to fuss, Gabi handed the baby to Stacey. Without missing a beat, Jude took Gabi's arm and announced he was giving her a grand tour of the buffet.

Before she knew what was happening, she was halfway across the room with the charming cowboy.

"A grand tour of the buffet?" Gabi slanted a playful glance in his direction. "Seriously?"

"Improv isn't my strength." Jude looked faintly embarrassed. "But sometimes there's only so much family a man can take. I'd like us to get better acquainted. We can't do that with everyone listening to our every word."

"Or your sister making gagging noises?"

He laughed. "That can be a deterrent."

"It's strange."

"What is?"

"Running into you this morning." She kept her tone light. "Now here."

"Fate," he said.

"Perhaps." She traced a finger around the rim of her glass and watched his eyes darken.

Without a word, he took her elbow, maneuvered her around several older couples sharing appetizers and conversation.

By the time he spoke again, the darkness in his eyes had lifted. "How is your father?"

"Much better," she told him. "Thank you for asking."

"It was a sacrifice for you to come all the way to Texas to be with him."

It was a statement, not a question.

"Nothing could have kept me away."

"As it should be" was all he said.

The conversation shifted to her life in Miami. Gabi kept it brief when telling him about her job at the bank. Though she enjoyed her work, she'd learned real estate lending wasn't all that interesting to those outside of the industry. She sipped her ginger ale. "What is it you do, Jude?"

"I have a ranch not far from here." Jude took a pull from his beer. "I do whatever needs to be done."

Though he shrugged, the pride in his voice told her he was one of the lucky ones who'd found his passion.

She'd opened her mouth to ask about his duties when one of his brothers—Christopher?—walked by and deliberately pushed Jude against her.

Jude's arm shot out, slipping around her, steadying them both.

For a second Gabi thought she heard Christopher laugh, but then the outside world disappeared as she gazed into Jude's eyes.

"Sorry 'bout that," he said, his gaze never leaving hers.

She swallowed and found her voice. "I'm not."

He grinned. "Hell, I'm not, either."

Yet she noticed he took a step back.

Gabi tried to collect her rioting thoughts. *Say something,* she told herself, *get the conversation back on safe ground.* She found herself blurting out the first thing that came to mind. "You grew up in Horseback Hollow?"

"I did." A twinkle filled his eyes, as if he could read her mind and found her unsteadiness amusing.

"Do you plan to stay?" Her tone held a hint of coolness. Gabriella Mendoza drooled over no man, at least not so he could notice.

"I like it here." He took a barely perceptible step forward. "Lubbock is close and with the recent growth in Vicker's Corners, there's enough to do."

"I guess I'll have to take your word. I haven't had the chance to do much exploring."

"I'd be happy to show you around."

She gave a little laugh, took another sip of her drink. "I wasn't hinting for a tour guide."

"I know." His eyes met hers and then slid

downward to linger on her mouth. "But since I'm already taking you on a tour of the buffet, why stop there? Let's take it a step further."

Gabi arched a brow, touched the tip of her tongue to her lips and watched his eyes change. "A step further?"

"Have dinner with me tomorrow night." Although his eyes burned, his smile was easy. "I'll introduce you to Horseback Hollow's culinary delights."

"I appreciate the offer." Gabi hesitated, sorely tempted. While it would be fun to spend time with Jude, the reason she was in Texas was to be with her father.

For a second the cowboy looked nonplussed. She guessed he wasn't used to being turned down. Not that she'd said no. She just hadn't said yes.

"You have to eat." His tone turned persuasive. "Surely you can spare an hour to become better acquainted with our town?"

With me.

Though he didn't say the words, Gabi knew what he was asking. She had to admit the short time she'd spent with Jude had only whet her appetite for more.

It wasn't as if she had to spend every waking second at her father's bedside, Gabi reminded herself. Taking a bit of time to get better acquainted with the town where her father lived *might* be a good idea.

But when she smiled and gave Jude Fortune Jones her answer, it wasn't getting acquainted with the town on her mind, it was getting better acquainted with her Texas cowboy.

Chapter 3

"I'm going to marry her," Jude told Liam, pointing across the room with his bottle of Dos Equis. "She's The One."

His older brother glanced out over the crowd, settling on... Delaney. "Uh, you're marrying our sister?"

"Not her." Jude spoke through gritted teeth. "The one next to her."

"The pretty Latina." Interest filled Liam's eyes. "She's a looker, all right. I wouldn't mind getting her between the sheets—"

Jude punched his brother in the shoulder. Hard. "Watch it. That's my future wife you're talking about."

Liam snorted. "Heard that one before."

"Heard what?" Sawyer sauntered up and handed Liam a beer.

"Jude says he's found The One." Liam laughed. "More like The One This Week."

Sawyer looked perplexed, but Jude saw no need to enlighten the cousin he'd only recently met. By the gleam in Liam's eyes, his brother didn't feel the same constraints.

"My brother here—" Liam gestured with his head toward Jude "—falls in love with every pretty filly that crosses his path. And just as quickly out of love. A guy could get whiplash watching him."

Obviously intrigued, Sawyer cocked his head. "Who is it this time?"

"Gabriella Mendoza." Jude let the name roll off his tongue. The name was as pretty as the woman. "I'm going to marry her."

"Ah, didn't the two of you just meet tonight?" Sawyer asked cautiously.

"Actually we ran into each other at the Superette this morning." Jude smiled, recalling how pretty she'd looked with the sun glinting off her walnut-colored hair. "Love at first sight."

"It's a little faster than normal," Liam informed Sawyer as if Jude wasn't standing right there. "I'm figuring it's the hearts and flowers in the air, what with Stacey getting engaged and Valentine's Day drawing near."

"Scoff all you want," Jude told his brother. "She's The One."

"She's a nice woman," Sawyer said cautiously. "And very attractive."

"I'm taking her to dinner tomorrow."

Surprise flicked across Sawyer's face. "You move fast."

"I figure why waste time?" Jude took a long pull of beer. "When you know what you want and you find it...you go after it."

Gabi spent most of the next morning at the rehabilitation hospital, observing her father's therapy sessions. With an arm broken on one side and a leg broken on the other, it was difficult for Orlando Mendoza to even get up from the chair much less manage what the nurses called his ADLs—activities of daily living.

But her dad was tough. A man didn't survive all those years as an air force pilot and raise five kids without survival instincts. Gabi had lunch with him in the dining room down the hall from his room. Apparently the nurses believed in keeping the patients out of their rooms as much as possible.

"This is tasty." Gabi glanced down at the grilled chicken breast, brown rice and asparagus spears.

"It's exactly what you should be eating." Orlando spoke in the fatherly tone he took on when he was poised to lecture. "I hope you didn't have alcohol last night."

Gabi thought of the blended margaritas, the fine wine, even the bottles of Dos Equis. She shook her head. "You know I don't drink."

"You had a cup of coffee with you when you came yesterday."

"It was decaffeinated." Gabi held on to her growing frustration with both hands, reminding herself that her dad had a lot of time to worry. Even when he'd been busy, worrying about her and her health had been his favorite pastime.

"Oh," he said. "Good."

"I know how to take care of myself, Papi." She kept her tone gentle as she brought her hand to her chest. "This heart was a precious gift. I don't take it for granted."

"You were so sick." Her father's dark eyes took on a distant look. "Your mamma and I thought we were going to lose you. Barely more than a baby and we thought we would lose you."

Those dark days had occurred when Gabi was nineteen, hardly a baby by anyone's standards, unless by overprotective parents.

"You always pushed yourself too hard." He shook his head. "I told you many times to slow down but you wouldn't listen."

"It was a *virus*. From the stomach flu," Gabi

reminded him. "It didn't have a thing to do with my college schedule or my extracurricular activities."

The virus had attacked her heart. She thought she was on the road to recovery after a particularly bad few days of a GI bug that was making its way across campus until she became short of breath. The next day she landed in the ICU.

She almost died. That's what her parents told her. The doctors said her heart was so badly damaged a transplant was her only hope. Because of her grave physical condition she'd moved to the top of the transplant list.

Miraculously a heart had come her way. Now a heart that had once beat in another young person's chest pumped in hers. She meant it when she told her father she didn't take it for granted. Not for one second. When her cardiologist had told her no drinking, smoking or caffeine, she'd listened.

She knew other transplant patients who rebelled against the restrictions, but Gabi felt best when she ate right, exercised and followed doctor's orders. Still, her parents worried. Now that it was just her father, he worried double.

"I love you, *mija*."

The emotion so evident in his voice, in his eyes, melted away the annoyance. "Ditto. Now, if you're not going to eat that green Jell-O, hand it over."

Her father laughed and pushed the gelatin in front of her. "Hopefully they'll have red this evening. That's my favorite. And yours, if I remember correctly."

Gabi paused, a forkful of chicken hovering just outside her mouth. "About tonight. I plan to stay most of the day, but I won't be eating dinner with you."

Her father lowered his glass of milk.

"I'm going to check out The Horseback Hollow Grill this evening," she told him.

"I've eaten at The Grill," Orlando said slowly.

"What's it like?" Gabi kept her tone light and offhand.

"Like King's," he said, referring to a hamburger and hot dog place not far from his home in Miami. "Their specialty is grilled cheese sandwiches. I like them with jalapenos."

"Guess what I'm wearing will be good enough." Gabi glanced down at her jeans and sweater. As her father continued to stare, she forced a chuckle. "I'm excited about the prospect of becoming better acquainted with Horseback Hollow. That way, when I go back to Miami and you talk about different places, I can visualize them."

The tight set to her father's shoulders eased. "That makes sense. But eating alone can't be fun for you."

"Don't tell me you haven't eaten alone since moving here?"

"I have," he grudgingly admitted. "Perhaps Laurel could—"

"Laurel is busy with her new husband and the flight school." Gabi spoke quickly before her father could pull out his phone and call his boss. She lowered her fork to the plate. "Besides, I'm not going alone. Jude Fortune Jones, Sawyer's cousin, generously offered to show me around town."

For several long seconds, accompanied by the thumping of her heart, Orlando said nothing. He chewed, swallowed then took another sip of milk. "I've met Jude."

Gabi lifted a brow. "And?"

"He appears to be very popular with the ladies."

The sharp stab of jealousy that struck Gabi took her by surprise. But she merely smiled. "Good. Then he should be an excellent dinner companion."

"I don't want you getting involved with him."

Her father's vehemence surprised Gabi. "Why? Is there something you haven't told me?"

"You have a job in Miami. A good one."

"That's true," Gabi agreed. "And once you're better, I'll be returning to that good job. In the meantime, I'd like to do a little exploring. With someone local."

Gabi finished her lunch and stayed for several more hours, watching her father work with the physical therapist on transferring from the bed to the chair. She listened as the occupational therapist showed him ways to use his left hand to do everything from getting toothpaste on his toothbrush to slipping on a shirt.

By the time the OT left, her father's eyes were drooping and his primary nurse suggested a nap.

"I'll be back after dinner." Gabi brushed a kiss across his leathery cheek and felt a surge of love.

"Lloyd and I have a date to play poker," he told her. "There's no need to drive back tonight. Enjoy your evening."

"Are you sure?"

"You spent all day here," he said. "Besides, I need to win some money off Lloyd, and I can't do that with someone breathing over my shoulder."

Gabi smiled. "Okay, then."

"Don't have the grilled cheese." This time the fatherly tone brooked no argument. "Too much fat in it."

Gabi simply smiled, gave a little wave and left him to his nap.

The knock on the front door of her father's small home sounded at precisely 6:00 p.m.

Gabi smiled. Apparently, the man was not only pretty to look at, but punctual, as well. *Popular with the ladies.* Some of her pleasure dimmed before she shoved the thought aside.

It didn't matter to her if Jude dated a different woman every night. This was simply dinner and conversation. She didn't expect more. Didn't want more.

When the knock sounded again, she sauntered across the room. After glancing through the peephole, she pulled the door open.

"I appreciate a man who's on time." With a welcoming smile she waved him inside.

Dressed simply in jeans, chambray shirt and a battered leather jacket, he whipped off his Stetson when he stepped through the doorway then thrust out one hand. "These are for you."

"Thank you." She glanced down at the bouquet he offered. Startled surprise quickly gave way to sweet pleasure. "Daisies are one of my favorite flowers. Have a seat. I want to put them in water before we leave."

She took the flowers into the small kitchen at the back of the house. Instead of sitting in the living room as she'd directed, he followed her.

"Nice place."

Gabi tried to see it through his eyes. White painted cupboards, grey Formica countertops, speckled linoleum flooring. Perfect, if a person was into retro decor. "My father feels at home here," she said. "Our home in Miami was bigger, but since it's just him, he doesn't need much space."

"The fact it's not large and all on one level should make it easier for him when he comes home."

"Good point." She rummaged through the cupboards, finally pulling out a red vase. "This will be perfect."

Her mother had collected red glass, and this little cylindrical vase had been a favorite. She quickly filled it with water then took a second to arrange the flowers.

"You have a knack," Jude commented from where he stood with his back resting against the doorjamb. "My mother does, too. If it were me, I'd stuff them into a vase and call it good."

Gabi took a step back and gazed in satisfaction at the arrangement. "They're too pretty to treat in that manner."

"They're pretty." Jude's husky voice did strange things to her insides. "But not as pretty as you."

She smiled. Oh, yes, he was a smooth one.

"Do I need a coat?" she asked, looking at his leather jacket.

"It's in the forties, so I say definitely." He paused. "Do you have one?"

"I didn't," she told him. "There was no need in

Miami. But I went shopping recently in Vicker's Corners and picked one up."

In fact, that's where she'd purchased the crimson sweater and black pants she wore now. From all signs, the small town in between Horseback Hollow and Lubbock was experiencing a growth spurt. She'd seen signs advertising new condominiums and touting luxury estates for sale.

"What'd you think of VC?" he asked as they moved to the living room, where she retrieved her coat from the postage-stamp-size closet.

"I liked it." She thought of the cute little business district with all the eclectic shops lining the main street. "But Horseback Hollow is nice, too."

"If I had to compare the two—" with well-practiced ease, Jude took the coat from her hands and held it up "—I'd say Horseback Hollow is the Jones family while Vicker's Corners is more like their gentrified relatives."

"Would those gentrified relatives be the Fortunes?" Gabi tried to ignore the brush of his knuckles against the side of her neck as he helped her slip on the coat.

"Bingo."

"Your mother recently found out she was related to the Fortunes, isn't that right?" Gabi tried to remember what her father had said, but the comment had been something he'd tossed out in passing and she hadn't given it much thought.

"That's right." He waited for her to pick up her purse then opened the front door and stepped to the side.

Good-looking. Manners. A powerful combination.

As she passed him, Gabi caught a faint whiff of his cologne. First he brought her flowers, now he wore the scent that had tantalized and enticed her last night. Jude Fortune would be a difficult man to resist.

Which she would, but that didn't mean she couldn't enjoy his company and the way he smelled. "You added Fortune to your name."

"My mother asked." Jude lifted one shoulder in a shrug. "She doesn't ask for much."

Gabi walked by his side to the truck parked in the driveway and tilted her head, thinking of her father. "What did your dad think? Mine is so proud of the Mendoza name that I can't imagine him being happy if any of my brothers decided to make a change."

Jude waited to answer until she stepped inside the truck. "Like most of us, he finds it difficult to deny her anything."

As he rounded the front of the massive vehicle, then got behind the wheel, Gabi thought of her mother. Her dad had loved his wife totally, completely. If there had been something important her mother had asked of him, he'd have gone along.

Jude slanted a sideways look. "Red is definitely your color."

A ripple of pleasure passed over Gabi. "I like your style, Jude."

He grinned and backed the truck out of the driveway. "Tell me about Gabriella."

On the short drive to the café, Gabi filled him in. She talked about her brothers and what it was like growing up as the youngest and the only girl. When he pressed for more, she told him she'd had a love for the business world since she'd opened her first lemonade stand at age five and made ten dollars.

"It didn't sink in until years later that my only customers had been relatives and close neighbors." Gabi chuckled. "I thought it was this great spiel I had going that drew them in."

"You enjoy your job."

"I do. Though the banking industry has taken some hits, the one I work for has done well." Gabi rolled her window partially down and let the fresh air waft into the cab of the truck. "It smells so fresh here."

"I bet this has been a bit of culture shock for you."

"Since I haven't seen a bodega or a palm

tree in weeks, I'd say that's an accurate statement." Gabi wondered how she could feel so relaxed around a man she'd just met. She'd been on plenty of first dates, and they were usually awkward, tense affairs. "Still, something about this place feels like home. I had difficulty understanding when my father told me how much he liked it here. Now it makes sense."

Jude wheeled the truck into an angled parking spot and cut the engine. "I hope dinner tonight only solidifies that impression."

Seconds later, Gabi stood in the doorway of The Horseback Hollow Grill, affectionately called The Grill by locals, and felt the first twinge of unease. Although clean, the tiled flooring had more than a few cracks. Artificial flowers in hammered coffee pots sat on tables. The tables reminded Gabi of the type you'd see in old-time diners, rounded edges encased in silver metal.

Jude inhaled deeply. "It always smells good in here."

Gabi could almost see onion rings swimming in a grease pool and hamburgers being flipped on the grill. Her head may have told her to run to the nearest deli for a turkey sandwich on whole wheat—hold the mayo—but her stomach had other ideas. It growled. Loudly.

Jude grinned. "Someone is ready to eat."

"I may be a little hungry" was all Gabi said as the hostess directed them to a booth by the front window.

"I can vouch for the burgers." Jude waited until she'd slid into the booth before taking a seat opposite her. "Half pound of pure Angus. My sisters are especially fond of the grilled cheese sandwich, which is a specialty."

Because of her heart, Gabi limited the amount of red meat she consumed as well as avoiding fried foods. She could already see there wasn't much on the menu that would get a cardiologist's seal of approval. Tonight she'd simply have to wing it.

Jude kept the conversation light and entertaining until the pretty blonde waitress arrived to take their orders. He seemed oblivious to the young woman's attempts to flirt. Fixing his eyes on Gabi's, he smiled. "Have you decided?"

"I'll have the hamburger." Gabi shifted her gaze to the blonde. "Well-done, please. May I substitute a salad for the fries?"

When the woman nodded, Gabi smiled. "Vinegar and oil for the dressing, on the side."

Jude ordered the hamburger and fries. When the waitress left, he told Gabi, "You can have some of my fries. They're the best."

"I might take you up on that offer," she said, relieved to have made it through the ordering without a lot of explanation. Though she wasn't ashamed of having had the transplant, she'd noticed that people often treated her differently once they knew. "I told you everything about me on the drive over. Now it's your turn to dish."

"I hardly think you told me everything," he said, "in a five-minute drive."

Though his tone was teasing, Gabi froze. She hadn't thought her father had mentioned the transplant to anyone, but she didn't know that for sure. "What did I leave out?"

"You didn't say anything about a man in your life." He took the iced tea the waitress gave him while Gabi slipped a straw into her ice water.

"That's because there is no man in my life," Gabi said honestly.

"I find that difficult to believe."

"It's true." Gabi thought back to Tony, the IT manager from the bank, and the horrified look on his face when he'd seen her scar. She shrugged. "Work takes most of my time."

"Their loss is my gain." Jude reached across the table and took her hand, bringing it to his lips. The feel of his mouth against her skin brought a rush of desire as unexpected as it was pleasant.

Gabi wasn't a neophyte, though she was hardly experienced, either. During her twenty-six years she'd only had two lovers: her high school boyfriend on prom night and a fellow business student in college.

The prom night had been a disaster. A car was not the place for lovemaking.

The relationship with her college boyfriend had taken place over most of her freshman year. He'd been fairly experienced, but looking back, Gabi could see now that he'd been more concerned with his own pleasure than with hers. Still, she'd enjoyed their time together and had believed he cared about her.

Then she'd gotten sick. He'd come a couple of times to the hospital, but by the time she was feeling better, he was out of her life.

"Tell me about Jude." Gabi fought to keep her voice steady, no easy task since her body had begun to vibrate.

"Not much to tell." He lowered her hand to the table and casually laced his fingers through hers. "I got my BA from Tech and I've worked on the ranch since I was old enough to hop on a horse."

"Have you ever thought of moving away? Trying something new?"

His blue eyes grew thoughtful. "A few times. But like my daddy, I love what I do. I like the variety and being my own boss. Horseback Hollow might be small, but it's a cohesive community and Lubbock is just down the road. Vicker's Corners is even closer."

"Sounds like we've both chosen the right path...for us." He continued to hold her hand, and the feel of his warm skin against hers sent her thoughts careening down a road she had no intention of traveling. Gabi was relieved when the waitress appeared with a mountain of food and he sat back.

"Oh, my." She gazed at a burger as big as her plate and a salad big enough for three to share.

Jude grinned. "I told you the food here is the best."

Gabi carefully considered for a moment then removed the hamburger from the sesame bun.

"Wimp." Jude stopped, looked stricken. "Sorry."

"No worries." Waving a dismissive hand, Gabi stole one of his fries. "I simply prefer to enjoy the meat."

In the end, she ate half of her burger and a third of the salad and sat back, satisfied.

"They have great sundaes here." Jude spoke in a persuasive tone when the waitress had cleared their plates.

Though she wouldn't mind having a spoonful, she doubted her stomach could handle even one more bite. "I'm so full you're going to have to roll me out of here as it is. But, if you'd like dessert, go ahead."

"I've had enough to eat," he said. "But I

wouldn't mind taking a walk. Are those boots you're wearing—"

"They're very comfortable." Gabi brightened at the realization Jude didn't seem in any hurry to have the evening end. "I'd love some fresh air."

Gabi pulled out her wallet to pay her share of the tab, but Jude had already handed the waitress several bills and told the blonde to keep the change.

"I can pay for my own."

"You could." He slid from the booth. "But tonight is my treat."

Gabi slipped out from her side, and when she stood, he was right there, holding out the coat that she'd hung on a metal hook at the edge of the booth.

He took her arm as they stepped out into the cool night air. They walked down the sidewalk, the full moon hanging like a large golden orb in the clear sky overhead.

"Thank you for the dinner," Gabi said again.

"You didn't eat much."

"It was good." She gazed into his eyes and had to resist the urge to reach up on her tiptoes and plant a kiss on those full lips. "I enjoyed it."

His eyes locked on hers. She saw them darken. Held her breath as he took a step forward and lowered his head to hers.

Chapter 4

Jude slipped his arms around Gabi's slender frame and watched her eyes close. His mouth skimmed the edge of her jaw, testing the sweetness of her skin. He nuzzled her neck then found himself shoved off balance from behind.

Irritation spiked. Jude whirled. If Chris was screwing with him again, his brother wouldn't find him so understanding this time.

"Sorry 'bout that, dude," the young shaggy-haired cowboy called over his shoulder as he lurched down the sidewalk, laughing with his friends, all three men obviously intoxicated.

When Jude turned to Gabi, he discovered she'd taken a step back. Just a small one, but enough to tell him the moment had passed. Still, the heat simmering in the air practically guaranteed there'd be another moment, another opportunity, before the night ended.

"There are so many out tonight." Gabi gestured toward the business district. People stood in front of the Superette, the saloon and The Grill. They talked, flirted, and one couple kissed as if no one else in the world existed.

The same way he'd felt only moments ago, Jude realized.

"I didn't know this many people lived in Horseback Hollow," Gabi said.

"It's Saturday night and unseasonably warm." Jude raised a hand in greeting to several ranch hands then refocused on Gabi's beautiful face. "Most of the cowboys from nearby ranches come into town to eat, drink and dance."

Her eyes went round as quarters. "Dancing? Really? Where?"

"The Two Moon Saloon," Jude said, mentioning the business adjacent to The Grill. "The owners bring in bands on Saturday nights. In fact—" he glanced at his phone "—the party should be getting started anytime now."

"I like to dance." A wistful look crossed Gabi's face. "Salsa mainly."

"We mostly two-step around here."

She inclined her head, her brown eyes thoughtful. "Is it difficult to two-step?"

The way she looked at him told Jude she could be persuaded to prolong the date…if dancing was part of the package.

"Naw." He took her arm. "Easy. Want to give it a try?"

After a second's hesitation, she nodded. "Sure. Sounds like fun."

He looped an arm companionably around her shoulders as they walked. "Have I told you I like a woman with an adventurous spirit?"

Gabi simply laughed, the moon scattering light on the dark hair that hung past her shoulders.

As Jude expected, the place was packed. He'd hoped to find a quiet table in a corner where he and Gabi could be alone when they weren't on the dance floor. But the second he walked in and saw friends and relatives scattered throughout the bar, he knew there would be no alone time. Not this evening.

They ended up at a table with two of his brothers and several ranch hands. When one of the cowboys kept talking to Gabi, Jude gave the guy a dark glance, making it clear the lady was with him.

But was she? Though Gabi didn't flirt with the other men, she also didn't cling to him. It was almost as if they *were* buddies, out for a night on the town together.

If that's the way she wanted it, he'd be her buddy. In time, they'd be more. He hadn't been kidding when he'd told Liam and Sawyer she was The One. The moment she'd run into him, he recognized her as the woman he'd been waiting for his whole life. Corny, but true.

When the band began to play a current country classic, he grabbed her hand and pulled her to the dance floor. As predicted she picked up the steps easily. Two quick. Two slow.

"You're doing great. That's it." Approval mixed with the encouragement in his tone. "Let your feet glide."

Gabi had a natural sense of rhythm. Her lithe but curvy body surprised him with some great moves within the simple step. As they danced, her cheeks flushed with color and her smile flashed often.

The band took a brief break, and he and Gabi were on their way back to the table when they ran across Sawyer and Laurel. While Gabi chatted with them, Jude excused himself.

When he returned, her head jerked up at the Richie Ray tune that the band had begun to play.

"That's salsa music." Delight filled her eyes even as they narrowed suspiciously. "Did you have anything to do with this?"

"Do you want to stand here and talk?" he asked then held out a hand. "Or shall we dance?"

"You can salsa?" Delight filled her voice.

In answer, he led her to the dance floor and proceeded to show her some of his moves.

The night passed quickly. Jude couldn't remember the last time he'd had so much fun or danced to so many songs. By the time she grabbed his arm and pulled him from the dance floor, his breath came in short puffs.

Gabi's own breath wasn't all that steady. "I think I'm going to call it a night."

Her cheeks were pink and her lips reminded Jude of a plump, ripe strawberry from his mother's summer garden. She looked so pretty, and he wanted her so badly that he almost kissed her right then, in front of half the citizens of Horseback Hollow.

Then he remembered what Sawyer had said about her father being overprotective. If Jude Fortune Jones kissed Orlando Mendoza's daughter on the dance floor of the Two Moon Saloon, news would be all over town by morning.

And even some sixty miles away in Lubbock, before Orlando finished his breakfast, someone would mention the incident to him. There was no reason to get the man stirred up when he was trying to recover. Besides, the way Jude saw it, what happened between him and Gabi was personal. That's how he preferred to keep it. For now.

Gabi paused at the edge of the dance floor, leaning close to ensure he could hear her over the twang of the steel guitar. "My father's house isn't far so—"

"Hey, Jude." A leggy redhead he'd dated last summer sidled up to him, her fingers traveling up his sleeve. "I got the band to promise they'd do the electric slide next. Told them it's our song."

"Sorry, Lissa." He put his hand on the small of Gabi's back. "We were just leaving."

Gabi opened her mouth as if to protest, but he closed it with a brief, hard kiss.

His pretty Latina's long lashes fluttered, and when he pulled back, she appeared slightly dazed.

"Oh." Lissa frowned, her gaze shifting between Jude and Gabi. "I saw you dancing, but I didn't realize you two were together, together."

"We are. Great seeing you, Lis." Without giving the redhead a chance to respond to his pronouncement, he took Gabi's arm and propelled her out the front door.

Once they reached the sidewalk, Gabi dug in her heels. "Stay. Dance with your friend. My father's house isn't far. I can walk myself home."

"Not alone."

The flat quality to his voice must have raised red flags. Concern filled her eyes. "Isn't it safe?"

"It's not that." No matter how much Jude wanted her to stay with him and not take off on her own, he refused to lie. "You'd be perfectly safe. The fact is, I'm not nearly ready for the night to end."

"Oh," she said, then again. "Oh."

"Unless this is your way of saying it's been fun but it's time for me to get lost?"

Gabi slowly shook her head and the tight knot in his belly dissolved. She rested her hand on his biceps. "I enjoy being with you."

"Good." He tucked her fingers more firmly around his arm.

In no particular hurry, they strolled down the sidewalk, soon exchanging the noise and lights of the downtown district for an occasional barking dog. Still warm from the dancing, Jude let his coat hang open.

Gabi kept hers firmly cinched around her waist. Thin blood from the hot Florida weather, he decided.

Jude gently locked his fingers with hers. Their hands swung slightly between them as they walked. For a second, he could see his parents strolling down the lane in the evening after supper, holding hands in companionable silence.

He and his siblings had thought it strange. For the first time, though, he understood that contentment. Feeling the warmth of Gabi's hand against his, seeing her face bathed in moonlight, he was happy sharing this moment with her, simply being with her.

They were almost to her father's house when out of the corner of his eyes, he saw her lips twitch. "Something funny?"

"Just remembering my high school days." She gave his hand a squeeze and smiled. "Back then my father would be waiting up for me with the porch light blazing."

Her dad didn't sound much different than the fathers of some of the girls he'd dated in high school. "I bet he'd miraculously appear on the porch just as you and your guy reached the steps."

Your guy.

Jude didn't like the sound of that, then reminded himself that while someone else may have been the first to kiss her, to caress, to make love with her…he would be the last.

"He wouldn't immediately appear." Gabi offered a wry smile. "Once the car hit the driveway, I had, oh, thirty seconds to get inside before the light began to flash. If I ignored that warning, he'd come outside."

"Half a minute doesn't give much chance to say good-night," Jude observed.

"Any good-night kissing had to be done before

I got home." Gabi grinned then sobered. "Not that I dated all that much."

"That surprises me."

"Why?"

"You're pretty," he said honestly, knowing the word didn't do justice to her beauty. Long, dark, wavy hair and big brown eyes. A slim, compact body with curves in all the right places. A smile that arrowed straight to his heart. "I'd have thought the boys would be flocking around."

"Two words." She exhaled a sigh and wiggled four fingers. "Older brothers."

Jude thought of Stacey and Delaney. He and his brothers had considered it their mission to protect their sisters from predatory males. "I can relate."

"I bet you can." Gabi rolled her eyes. "Because of my brothers and my dad, most guys ended up dropping me off in front of our house and speeding away."

Cowards, Jude thought with disgust. "I'd have insisted on walking you to the door."

"Then you're one in a million, Jude."

"I'm happy you recognize my worth." He shot her a wink as they climbed the stairs of her father's porch. "Seriously, my brothers and I were taught it was our responsibility to see our dates safely to the door."

When she stopped and turned back to him

without opening the door, Jude's heart slammed against his ribs. Stealing a quick kiss in the saloon was one thing. But with those unreadable dark eyes staring up at him now…

Jude had been dating since he was fifteen. So why did he feel as unsure as he had when he'd been about to kiss a girl for the first time? It made no sense. Other than Gabi was different and he didn't want to screw up.

The air grew thick, so thick he had difficulty breathing. The world around them faded away. All that existed was her. All that mattered was her.

Take it slow. Don't rush her.

The warning in his head stemmed from good, cold logic. She wasn't going anywhere, at least not soon. Her father had only recently been moved to rehab. They had plenty of time to build a relationship. For her to see, to accept, to embrace that he was her future husband.

Yes, he decided, he should take a step back. He'd been impulsive in the saloon. He needed to keep his desire for her under tighter control. There would be other opportunities, other nights for another kiss. A lifetime.

Dropping hands to his side, Jude kept his gaze on her eyes and away from those luscious lips. "I had a good time tonight."

Something that looked like disappointment

flashed in her eyes. Her brows pulled together. "Do you have something against kissing?"

He stared, nonplussed. "No. Do you?"

"Not if I like the guy." She gave him a long stare that fried every brain cell he possessed. "Not if he likes me."

"I like you." The second the words left his lips, Jude realized he *had* reverted back to his teenage self. Except he'd never been this lame.

"Happy to hear it." Her arms wound around his neck. "For a second I wondered if I'd lost my appeal."

"Oh, darlin'." Jude wanted so much to pull her close, to fit her hips against his. He settled for resting his hands on her shoulders. "That's never going to happen. But I don't want to rush you."

"You kissed me in the saloon," she reminded him.

"Impulse." He shook his head. "Not very gentlemanly."

"I believe—" She brought a finger to her lips and pretended to consider. "No, I'm certain. Being a gentleman is highly overrated."

Jude brushed a strand of hair back from her cheek with the back of his hand. "I doubt Orlando Mendoza would agree with that sentiment."

She laughed, a silver tinkle of a sound that relaxed the tight muscles in his shoulders.

"True." She gazed up at him from beneath

lowered lashes. "But he's not here, is he? Besides, I make my own decisions."

She was right. What her father wanted didn't matter. With the moon illuminating her face, her eyes shining, all that mattered was her and him and the moment.

Jude lowered his mouth and touched her lips with his. She tasted like spearmint candy. He loved spearmint. He moved his hands down her arms then settled them on her waist.

"I like you, Gabi." He let the word hum between them. Her brown eyes darkened to black in the dimness, but he didn't need light to read her expression. Leaning over, he kissed the base of her jaw.

She brushed her lips against his cheek.

"I like you a lot," he murmured, twining strands of her hair loosely around his fingers.

"Jude." She spoke his name then paused, as if not sure what she wanted to say.

When her gaze met his, their eye contact turned into something more, a tangible connection between the two of them. Time seemed to stretch and extend.

Then she ran her hands up the front of his coat and leaned toward him.

He made a sound low in his throat then folded her more fully into his arms, anchoring her against his chest as his mouth covered hers. His hand flattened on her lower back, drawing her more tightly against the length of him.

He loved the way she smelled, an intoxicatingly sweet mixture of perfume and soap. Loved the way she tasted. Spearmint.

"You are beautiful," he whispered into her ear right before he took the lobe between his teeth.

Shivers rippled across her skin.

"You're soft," he continued as he kissed her below her ear, then down her throat.

"The scent of you drives me wild."

The honking of a car horn and wild teenage laughter with a loud male voice yelling, "Get a room," had Gabi jumping back and Jude stifling a curse.

They'd already been interrupted a couple of times this evening. Enough, Jude thought, was enough. But he reined in his irritation as the night took on a sudden chill. "Gabi—"

"The porch light has flickered," she said with a rueful smile. "It's time for me to go inside."

Damn.

Jude shot a murderous glance at the disappearing taillights. Then he staunched the emotion and met her gaze. "I want to see you again."

"It's a small town," she said in a tone he found a little too cavalier. "It's inevitable."

He put his hands on her shoulders. Firmly met her gaze. "I want to see you again."

Her cheeks went a little pink. "I don't do casual affairs, Jude. I won't be in town long enough for anything more."

Jude wasn't interested in a casual affair, either. He wanted the more, would have the more, but it was much too early for that discussion.

"I enjoy spending time with you," he said again, firmly. What had his father once told him, *Begin as you mean to go on?* "I'll be calling, asking to see you again."

To seal the promise, he kissed her again.

Chapter 5

Gabi swore her lips still tingled when she arrived at the rehabilitation center the next day to see her father. The newspaper lay on a dining room table when she walked in.

Her breath hitched when he gave her a big smile. Love flowed through her. Though she adored her brothers, they'd been a unit of four. She'd spent most of her time with her mother. And when her father was home, she'd been a daddy's girl.

"You're looking chipper." Gabi slid into the chair on the other side of the table.

"I could say the same about you." He studied her thoughtfully. "You've got color in your cheeks."

"I've been spending more time outdoors," Gabi admitted, thinking of the early-morning run she'd taken as the sun painted the sky shades of pink and orange. "Though I've had to bundle up. It's definitely not as warm as Miami."

Her father laughed. "Not yet anyway, but I hear it's supposed to hit sixty today, which is really good for this time of year."

"Actually, I like the cooler weather. And Horseback Hollow is a great little community," she told him. "I understand now why you're so happy here."

"I wasn't sure you'd be able to see it." Orlando appeared pleased by her admission. "There's not much for young folks to do."

"I enjoyed the barbecue Friday night." Gabi decided to avoid any talk of last night's activities with Jude. "I got to know Sawyer and Laurel better. Deke and Jeanne Marie seem like very nice people."

"Their daughter Stacey is the one who stayed with me until the rescue squad got there."

"I remembered you telling me that and made sure to thank her."

"Good girl." He gave an approving nod then his gaze grew shrewd. "You haven't mentioned how your date went last night."

"It wasn't a date." Gabi resisted the urge to squirm in her seat. She could have cheered when her tone came out casual and offhand as she'd intended. "We went to dinner at The Grill then did a little dancing at the Two Moon Saloon."

Her father took a sip of coffee, inclined his head. "Dinner. Dancing. Sounds like a date to me."

"We had a nice evening." Gabi lifted one shoulder, flashed a smile. "I learned how to two-step."

The nurse came in before Orlando could begin a full interrogation. By the time the RN finished checking his vital signs and administering his medications, the talk turned to family. Apparently Gabi's brother Cisco had called that morning, and he and Orlando had enjoyed a lengthy and pleasant conversation.

"Stacey and I were chatting about older brothers at the barbecue," Gabi said, then wondered if bringing up the Fortune Jones family was a mistake. "I believe she and Delaney had it worse. They had five older brothers. I just had four."

"Your mother loved her boys." A smile lifted Orlando's lips ever so slightly. "But she cried with happiness when she finally had a daughter."

Gabi's heart swelled. "I miss her."

"I do, too." He reached over and patted her hand. "It can't be easy for you now, being the only woman in a family of men."

"It's not that—" Gabi's phone began to play a

catchy Latin tune. She shot an apologetic look at her father. "Sorry. I thought I'd put it on vibrate."

"Get it," Orlando urged. "It may be important."

Without even glancing at the readout, she answered the call. "This is Gabi."

"Good morning, Gabi. This is Jude." The rich baritone sent a flood of warmth surging through her veins. "How's your day going?"

"It's good." Before she could check her reaction, her voice took on a slightly breathless quality. "I ran four miles this morning, did some housework, and now I'm going to have lunch with my father."

"How's he doing?"

Gabi slanted a glance at her father and found him unabashedly staring. In spite of his injuries, he looked strong enough to hop into a plane and soar into the wild blue yonder. Or stride onto a porch and stand between her and anyone of the opposite sex. "Better every day."

"Glad to hear it." Jude paused. "I won't keep you, but I plan to inspect the fence on the southern border of our property tomorrow. I'd like your company. We can take the horses out. The weather is supposed to be good."

When Jude had called her adventurous, Gabi considered that to be the supreme compliment. She'd been given a second chance at life. She was determined to embrace that life, to live to the fullest each and every day.

"Well, ah—" Gabi glanced at her father. Still staring. "I've never ridden a horse before."

"No worries." Jude chuckled. "We have a mare, Sweet Betsy, who's so gentle a two-year-old would be safe on her. I'll have her saddled and ready for you. Is nine too early for you?"

Gabi considered her father's schedule. Most of his therapies were in the morning when he was fully rested. If she and Jude were back by noon—and she couldn't think why they wouldn't be—she could come straight to the hospital and have lunch with her father.

"Nine works."

"I'll be by your house at—"

"There's no reason for you to drive into town to pick me up," Gabi told him. "I'll meet you at your place at nine."

"Actually, why don't we meet at my parents' ranch?"

"Sounds good." Gabi found herself smiling as she ended the call. She'd always wanted to ride a horse. It looked like now she was going to have that chance.

"You're riding a horse?"

Gabi's back automatically stiffened at the disapproval in her father's tone. For a second, she'd been so caught up in making plans she'd forgotten he was sitting there, sucking in every word.

"It should be fun." When the scowl on her father's face deepened, she added, "I bet most of the women around here ride."

"You're not from this area," he said pointedly. "And you have to be extra careful."

Gabi told herself not to go there, to simply let the subject drop. But her mouth seemed determined to open and get her into trouble. "Are you worried I'll fall? If you are, don't give it a second thought. Jude plans to saddle up Sweet Betsy for me. Supposedly this horse is so mild-mannered a two-year-old could ride her."

"Yes, I'm worried about you on a horse. You're a city girl." Her father spoke through gritted teeth. "But I'm even more worried about you falling for a man like Jude."

Gabi counted to five. Lifted a brow. "A man like Jude?"

"He's got a rep."

Without taking her eyes off her father, she leaned back in her chair, forced a casualness at odds with her hammering heart. "Tell me more."

"He likes women," Orlando said as if that explained it all.

"I'd say that's a good thing."

Her father made an impatient gesture with his

good hand. "From what I've heard he goes from woman to woman, doesn't stick."

A knife sliced into her belly and twisted. Jealousy, she realized. Ridiculous, considering she and the handsome cowboy had only recently met.

"Why would that be a problem?" Gabi lifted a brow. "I live in Miami and I'm not looking to relocate."

"I don't want to see you hurt."

The look in his eyes was one of love, and Gabi felt her irritation subside. "Papi." She covered his hand with hers. "Jude is simply being nice, showing me around the area. He's not looking for anything more than companionship. I'm not looking for more, either."

Her father narrowed his gaze. "Does he know of your condition?"

The quick, hot surge of temper took Gabi by surprise. "I don't have a *condition*," she snapped. "I've had a heart transplant. I'm all better now."

Or close enough. She was down to only two meds.

Not surprisingly, Orlando didn't back down. "Does he know?"

"This may surprise you, but I don't shout my medical history from the rooftops of every town I visit." Gabi pushed back her chair with a clatter and rose to her feet. "I'd appreciate it if you didn't, either."

She bent, kissed his leathery cheek and spoke briskly. Lunch would have to wait for another time. "I'll be back in a couple of hours. I'm going to run some errands, pick up a few things while I'm here in Lubbock."

"I love you, Gabriella." He grabbed her hand before she could move away. "Sometimes my love makes me a little overprotective."

"A *little?*" She paused. Sighed. "I love you, Papi, but you need to remember I'm a grown woman. I handle my own affairs."

"But your heart—"

"My heart—" Gabi spoke slowly and distinctly so there could be no misunderstanding "—is strong and healthy and all mine. You don't have to worry about me giving it away to a stranger and getting hurt."

The truth was she didn't plan on giving her heart away to any man. Not even one who was handsome as sin and wore a black Stetson.

Jude ran into Sawyer in Vicker's Corners, just as he finished loading supplies in the back of his pickup. When his cousin crossed the street, Jude shut the tailgate and lifted a hand in greeting.

"Looks like you're going to be busy." Sawyer

gestured with his head toward the truck. "Don't you know Sunday is the day of rest?"

"Not on a ranch." Jude kept his smile easy. Although he didn't know Sawyer well, so far he liked what he'd seen. He appreciated the way Sawyer and his wife had looked out for Gabi's father. How a boss treated those who worked for him said a lot.

"Past lunchtime. Have you eaten?"

Jude took off his Stetson and raked a hand through his hair. "Not yet. It's been one of those days."

"Me, either." Sawyer gestured toward a family-style restaurant on the corner. "Got time to grab a quick burger?"

Though there was plenty of work waiting for him back at the ranch, Jude didn't hesitate. A man had to eat, after all.

Because it was nearly two, the after-church crowd had cleared out long ago and the only people in the place were a couple of grizzled old cowboys playing checkers at a corner table.

The hostess led them to a table by the window.

"How's Orlando?" he asked, after Arlene, a retired schoolteacher-turned-waitress, had taken their order and brought the drinks.

"You'd know better than me." Sawyer leaned back and relaxed against the vinyl seat, downing a good portion of his iced tea in one gulp. "I was surprised to see you with Gabi last night."

Jude smiled and changed the subject. "How's the accident investigation coming? Is sabotage still on the table?"

Jude had heard all about the anonymous letters received at the post office. Letters alluding that what happened to Orlando could happen again if the Fortunes didn't pull up stakes in Horseback Hollow. He was grateful neither his brothers nor the ranch hands had brought up the letters at the bar when he'd been with Gabi.

Sawyer waited to answer until the waitress had set the food in front of them and was out of earshot. "The NTSB is still investigating. Until they file their report we won't know for sure."

Jude hefted the massive burger. "What's your take?"

Sawyer dipped a French fry into a puddle of ketchup. "I don't think so, but being part of a famous family does open you up to all sorts of things."

"That sucks."

"Sometimes." A speculative look crossed Sawyer's face. "Are you sorry you became a Fortune?"

Jude shifted uncomfortably in his seat, but Sawyer had always been honest with him. He could be no less. "It takes more than DNA to make people family."

"True enough." Sawyer popped a fry into his mouth. "Though I have to say when I saw you, I recognized you as a Fortune immediately."

Jude grinned and simply shrugged. No use denying it. Everyone commented on the physical resemblance between Jude and his cousin.

"Your brother Christopher doesn't seem to be having any problem adjusting to his new family," Sawyer said in a casual tone that Jude guessed was anything but casual.

"That so?"

Sawyer added more salt to his fries. "He's considering a move to Red Rock."

Jude kept his face expressionless. "First I heard."

The thought that Chris would leave Horseback Hollow to hook up with the Fortunes didn't shock Jude. Not as much as if Sawyer had told him one of his other brothers was considering the possibility.

At twenty-six, Chris was the youngest of the five boys and the only one who'd never taken to life on the ranch. From the time he'd been a little boy, he and their father had been at odds. If their dad said something was black, Chris would insist it was white.

Still, Jude had to wonder what his little brother was up to....

Jude shoved the speculation aside. He had no doubt he'd find out soon enough what Chris had up his sleeve.

"Back to Orlando." Jude took a drink of cola. "I know he's worked for you the past couple of months. Has he said much about his daughter?"

A trace of a smile lifted Sawyer's lips. "You mean about your future wife?"

"Scoff all you want." Jude met Sawyer's mocking gaze with a steady one of his own. "When Gabi is walking down the aisle straight toward me, you'll be eating those words."

"Okay, okay." Sawyer took another bite of burger. "I'm sure you know more than me. She's one of five kids. The mother died several years back. O is very protective of her, so watch your step."

Jude's fingers tightened around the glass of cola. "Watch my step?"

The words were so cold frost could have formed on them.

His cousin waved a dismissive hand, his fingers holding a French fry. "You know what I mean."

"I would never take advantage of Gabi." The words were said slowly, concisely and with an edge even Sawyer couldn't fail to notice. "I care about her too much."

"Good. Then Orlando won't be a problem."

Jude wasn't sure about that, but right now it didn't matter. His focus was on Gabi, on getting to know her and having her get to know him. Not everyone fell in love at first sight.

Until Gabi got to know him she couldn't love him. And love was essential if they were going to have a long and happy life together.

Chapter 6

Gabi decided riding Sweet Betsy was very much like sitting in a rocking chair. The chestnut-colored mare had one speed and that was slow. Nothing interested her, not the rabbits hopping across the field nor the cattle grazing nearby.

Wherever Jude's stallion went, the mare was content to go. Jude had smiled approvingly at Gabi's jeans, boots and long-sleeved shirt with a jacket for the ride. Because the sun shone bright, he'd plopped a hat on her head.

She was grateful to have it. The sky was blue without a trace of clouds. A slight breeze added to the pleasantness of the day.

Though there wasn't a palm tree in sight, Gabi found the openness of the landscape appealing.

Just like the man at her side. Gabi slanted a sideways glance at the handsome cowboy, with the roll of wire hooked to his saddle.

"Do you like banana bread?" Jude asked when they drew close to a large pond.

It was an odd question, but Gabi answered truthfully. "Who doesn't?"

"My mother made some this morning, and I brought a few slices with me." Jude shot her a wink and slipped off the back of his horse with an ease Gabi envied. "I could be persuaded to share."

"I'll start working on appealing to your altruistic side," Gabi declared. "Once I quit gazing longingly at terra firma."

Taking hold of the chestnut's reins, he assisted Gabi off the horse. She stood there for a moment, her hands resting on his muscular forearms.

"It feels odd," she murmured.

He grinned. "Being on solid ground again?"

"No." Gabi cast a wary glance at the pond where their horses now stood drinking. "Being this close to water and not being on alert."

Jude cocked his head.

"Back home, when you see water that isn't the ocean, you think snakes and alligators."

The look he shot her was clearly skeptical. "You're making that up."

"I'm not," she insisted. "The church I attend

in Miami has a couple of lakes on their property. They got rid of the gators once but had to bring them back. Know why?"

"No clue."

"The snake population exploded. They even got into the building."

He gave a disbelieving snort.

"Honest to God." She swiped a finger across her heart. "We brought the alligators back to keep the snakes under control. And not just any snakes, water moccasins, the deadliest of all."

Jude shook his head. "You like living in such a place?"

"It's been my home for as long as I can remember," she said simply. "But it doesn't feel that way so much since my mom died and my dad moved away."

A wave of sadness washed over her at the realization that her father's departure had changed everything. In an attempt to shake off the unwanted melancholy, she performed a couple of stretches then shook out her hands, which had been holding the reins in a death grip. By the time she straightened, her mood had lightened.

"I could have been a Texan," she announced.

If Jude was surprised by the out-of-the-blue pronouncement, it didn't show. "Could have been? Or could be?"

"Could have been," she repeated. "My father

and his brothers were born in Texas, but relocated to Florida when they were young."

He slapped his hat against his dusty jeans. "That explains it."

She lifted a brow.

"You're a natural on a horse," he told her. "You're a born cowgirl."

Gabi laughed.

The sound made Jude smile. She captivated him. As she had from the first moment he'd seen her.

"Where's my banana bread?" Gabi asked.

"I thought you were going to persuade me to share."

She stared at him for a long moment, a speculative gleam in her eyes. "What's it going to take?"

He simply smiled, enjoying the game.

"A little buttering up?"

He grimaced. "That makes me sound like a tub of popcorn at the movie theater."

She fisted her hands on her hips, considered. After a second, she took a step closer, slid her hands up his chest to the lapels of his shirt. "Oh, Jude," she simpered. "You're so handsome."

He cocked his head and stared pityingly at her.

She dropped her hands, frowned. "You're right, way too cliché."

"But you're on the right track," he admitted, making her smile.

"Okay." She took a deep breath, let it out slowly then tipped her head and gazed up at him through lowered lashes. Her voice became a sultry purr. "Have I told you that I absolutely adore your muscles?"

He appeared to consider then shook his head. "I don't believe you have."

"I do," she said, all wide-eyed and innocent. "I know some women go for the starving-poet look. You know—guys with that long shaggy hair and not a manly muscle in sight."

"I take it you're not one of them."

Gabi trailed a finger across his biceps, a hint of a smile curving her lips upward when the muscle jumped. "I prefer men who look like men. I like them gentle but strong. You know— the kind of man a woman can depend on."

She stopped, as if she'd taken it further than she'd intended. But Jude liked knowing that she found him attractive, that his body appealed to her. And since they were exchanging confidences…

"Have I told you the kind of woman who appeals to me?"

Gabi shook her head, a cautious look in her eyes.

"Short women with dark hair?"

"Not just any short woman with dark hair." He took a step closer. "You."

She inched back. "Ah, that's sweet."

"I mean it." He took her face in his hands and gave her a smile so warm it made something inside her ache. "I've dated women of all shapes and sizes and found many of them attractive. But none compare to you."

She feigned a look of mild interest. "Tell me more, smooth-talking cowboy."

"I speak the truth."

"Yeah, right."

"Seriously, I love the way your hair shines like dark walnut in the sun." He touched those silky strands as he spoke, marveling at the softness. "Your eyes remind me of the finest Venezuelan chocolate."

"They don't make chocolate in Venezuela."

He smiled. "They do. My mother received some as a gift for Christmas from Sawyer. I remember the rich, dark color. It was the first thing I thought of when I saw your eyes."

She blinked. "Well, thank you."

"And your body." His gaze slid up and down from the cowboy hat to the tips of her dusty boots. "You're small and muscular, but you have curves in all the right places. When you're against me we fit together perfectly. You fit me perfectly."

"If you were the one trying to convince me to give you a piece of banana bread, it'd already be on your plate."

Jude let his gaze linger on her lips. "I'm not hungry for banana bread."

Her dark eyes sparkled in the sunlight. She moistened her lips with the tip of her tongue.

"I admit I'm tempted to kiss you," she said in that sultry tone he found so incredibly sexy, "but I'm not into public displays of affection."

Confused, Jude glanced around to see who was riding up. But he saw only cows and pastureland. "We're the only ones here."

Gabi gestured with her head toward the herd of longhorns eyeing them suspiciously from behind a string of fence.

He grinned and shook his head. "They don't count."

"Maybe." When she looked like she might be thinking of making a run for it, Jude grabbed her hand and tugged her to him.

"Not so fast, darlin'," he said in a deep voice with the faintest hint of a Texas drawl. "First things first."

Gabi stood so close he could see the flecks of gold in the rich brown depths of her eyes.

"Oh, that's right." She gave a throaty laugh and batted those long lashes. "You owe me a slice of banana bread."

"I want to kiss you." His gaze met hers. "And you want to kiss me."

"I guess we might as well go ahead and lock lips." Though Gabi's voice had a slightly bored edge, the flicker of desire in her eyes gave her away. "It's not like we have anything better to do."

"We could eat the banana bread." He trailed kisses up her neck.

She arched back, giving him full access to her throat. "Too many fat grams."

He nibbled on her ear, inhaling the light floral scent of her perfume. "We'll stick with this, then."

"I thought you were going to kiss me." Her breath came in little puffs.

"I think that's what I'm doing," he said, nipping her shoulder through the fabric.

When his hands began to slide slowly upward, Gabi inhaled sharply, her body quivering.

"You haven't come close to my mouth," she said in a breathless tone.

"I'll be getting there, darlin', don't you worry."

When his mouth reached the V of her shirt and his tongue made contact with the hollow of her throat, she gasped.

He'd never seen a woman keep herself so covered up. But Jude had to admit it was enticing.

He couldn't wait to catch his first glimpse of the curves underneath all that fabric.

His hand slid up to cover her high firm breast, teasing the nipple through the thin cotton of the shirt. Her breath caught then released with an involuntary sound.

As he continued to lift, support and stroke her yielding flesh with his fingers, he closed his lips over hers, softly at first then slowly increasing the pressure. Soon he found himself kissing her as if she was water and he'd been in a desert. Which, in a way, was true.

Before her, there had been nothing. She filled him in a way no other woman had done. This was his future wife in his arms.

Her body hummed beneath his touch. The surprised wonder in her eyes when he hit a sensitive spot told him she didn't have a lot of experience. This was fine with him. But it meant he needed to go slow.

Going slow became increasingly difficult. The taste of her aroused him. Hunger struck against equal hunger, creating fire. As they continued to kiss, as he caressed her, the fire became an inferno. He cupped her and she whimpered, pressing up against his hand.

If Jude was only thinking of himself, he'd take the blanket off his saddle roll, shuck his clothes—and hers—and be rolling around on the ground in seconds. But he wanted the first time they made love to be special.

She melted against him, allowing his tongue to slip inside, just as he wanted to slip inside her.

As if reading his mind, she shifted slightly, opening her stance. They came together perfectly—two halves finally made whole—only separated by clothing.

When she began to shimmy against him, Jude had to fight to hold on to control.

Up. Down. Up. Down.

Her throaty cries made his blood burn hot.

Up. Down.

He envisioned her—wet, slick and ready beneath the denim.

Her breath came in little moans. Or were those sounds from his own throat? Could a man die from raw need? At the moment it seemed highly probable.

The sun burned hot overhead but Jude barely noticed. All he knew was Gabi and the feel of her soft body against the hard length of him.

Tension filled every muscle. He couldn't get enough of her. He dug his fingers into her hips and increased the rhythm. Faster. Her frantic response urged him faster still.

She strained toward him, reaching, needing, wanting.

Seconds later, her body convulsed in release.

She cried out, pressing hard against him, her eyes going blind. Still he continued. Up. Down. Slowly now—gentling the contact until the last bit of pleasure had been wrung from her body.

Until she went limp and collapsed in his arms with a shudder.

Once Gabi's brain became capable of forming a coherent thought, she realized anything she'd experienced before had only been a pale imitation of the real thing. She hadn't even gotten naked yet, but she'd experienced more passion and felt more satisfaction than she ever had before.

While Gabi had enjoyed her previous sexual encounters, she'd never been swept away in the moment. Yet, only a few seconds earlier, she'd been willing to do anything to ensure Jude kept touching her, kissing her.

She now stood cosseted in his arms, sated and content. A slight breeze ruffled her hair as she rested her head against his chest and listened to the comforting beat of his heart.

Gabi inhaled deeply. She loved the way he smelled—a woodsy mixture of cologne and soap and maleness that kept heat percolating low in her belly.

Jude's lips brushed the top of her head. "You," he said, "are amazing."

The feeling beneath his gentle tone and the answering emotion it aroused sent red flags popping up. How could she feel so close to a man she barely knew? Things were moving too fast and in a direction she couldn't afford to go.

If it was only the physical aspect drawing her to Jude, she'd be safe. But Jude Fortune Jones was the total package. Which was why it made sense to put a little distance between them. But when Gabi moved slightly back, he tugged her close.

Her fingers itched to reach between them, unzip his jeans and give him all the pleasure he'd so generously given to her. Then round two could begin, only this time sans clothing.

The mere thought of his talented fingers and mouth on her bare skin sent anticipation coursing up her spine and heat pooling between her thighs.

She'd let it go this far. What would be wrong with taking it all the way?

Yet, even as temptation beckoned, there were things they needed to settle first. She could be Jude's friend and even entertain the possibility of a friends-with-benefits relationship while she was in Horseback Hollow.

But she couldn't become involved in a serious relationship or plan a life with him. Not with her future so tenuous.

She'd witnessed firsthand the toll that losing her mom had taken on her father. It wouldn't be fair to fall in love, marry and knowingly put a man she loved in that same situation.

Though Gabi had done well since her surgery, she knew that could change without warning. She'd seen that happen with Mary and Kate, a couple of her transplant buddies.

While she may have told her father she was "all better" and didn't have a "condition," she knew she'd always be a heart patient. She'd always be on antirejection medication. And she'd always be at an increased risk of a health crisis that could take her life.

Of course, she might be making a big deal over nothing. Not all men who pursued a woman did it with a serious relationship or marriage in mind. If Jude was indeed a man who "liked the ladies," a few weeks of fun and sex before she returned to Florida could be all he was after.

If she knew that was his mindset, Gabi would rip off his clothes and have her way with him right now. Even the knowledge that the cows would get an eyeful wouldn't slow her down.

But what was going through his head was a mystery, so Gabi determinedly stepped from his arms and pretended sudden interest in straightening her clothing.

When she looked up, his blue eyes, so often

filled with good humor, reminded her of a stormy windswept sea. The expression on his face was serious as his eyes searched hers. "Are we good?"

It didn't take a rocket scientist to realize he wanted to know if their momentary interlude had screwed things up between them.

Easy-breezy, she told herself and smiled. "Stellar."

The tenseness eased from his shoulders, but a hint of worry remained in his eyes.

"The air between us was hot enough to combust." Jude shoved his hands into the pockets of his jeans. "I hadn't planned—"

"On a make-out session in front of the bovines?"

Jude laughed then cocked his head. "We could take it to the next level and really give them something to look at this time."

His wicked smile tempted, but she shook her head.

"You have to check on the fence," she reminded him, keeping her tone light, fighting for casual. "Besides, I'm in the mood to ride."

It sounded plausible. Practical. Believable.

If she could have kept her eyes from straying to the bulge below his belt buckle. *If* her breath hadn't hitched.

She heard him chuckle, jerked her head up.

The stormy eyes now held laughter and what she recognized as the hot glint of desire.

"A horse." She moved quickly to Sweet Betsy's side even as the image of *her* riding *him* painted bold, fiery strokes across her brain. "I want to ride a horse."

The knowing look in his eyes told her he wasn't fooled. "Need any help mounting the… horse?"

Gabi's throat went dry as dust. If he touched her now…

"Got it covered," she managed to croak before pulling herself up onto the mare with the ease of an experienced rider.

In seconds Jude was on the stallion. He shifted a bit as if trying to find a comfortable position.

Though it wasn't at all charitable, especially in light of how generous he'd been with her, Gabi stifled a snicker.

Instead of giving the horse a light tap of his heel, Jude stared with those enigmatic blue eyes, his gaze lingering on her mouth.

Gabi licked the lips that were now as dry as her throat.

As if satisfied, his molten gaze dropped to her chest. Her breasts had begun to tingle when his gaze lowered again.

One look was all it took. A river of heat rushed through her to settle at the apex of her thighs. She squirmed, trying to find a position that didn't intensify the ache between her legs.

The smile Jude shot her stopped just short of a smirk. Then he pressed his lower legs against the horse and took off across the field toward the fence line.

Now he wasn't the only one who wanted, the only one left with unrequited yearnings. As he disappeared over the ridge, Gabi realized with a pang that letting him ride away was exactly what she'd soon face.

But not today. Not yet.

She pressed her heels into Sweet Betsy's sides and raced after him.

Chapter 7

Gabi and Sweet Betsy reached the big red barn shortly before eleven. After the ranch hands took the horses, Jude invited Gabi into the house. He promised coffee to go with the slices of banana bread they had yet to eat.

A desire to stay warred with Gabi's need to leave and make sense of what had happened today. She was relieved she could honestly say her father expected her to join him for both lunch and dinner.

Disappointment skittered across Jude's face, but he walked her to the Buick like a gentleman, their interlocked fingers swinging easily between them.

The simple act only intensified the conflicting

emotions battling inside her. She wanted to see Jude again, wanted to touch and be touched by him. But considering the intensity of the emotions and desires he engendered, being close didn't seem wise.

She worried this was all a game to him. Yet, wasn't that what she wanted? She felt dizzy as possibilities spun and swirled in her head. Could she do easy-breezy with no strings? Did she have a choice?

Thankfully she had the hour drive to Lubbock to think, to plan, to decide where they went from here.

But when she tried to slip behind the wheel of the LeSabre, Jude blocked her with his arm, a pleasant smile on his lips, a watchful look in his eyes. "I want to see you again."

"I'm sure you will." She lifted a shoulder, not wanting to commit to any course of action until she'd thought things through. "Horseback Hollow is a small town. Our paths can't help but cross."

Confusion blanketed his face. It was obviously not the response he'd expected. "Are you angry with me about something?"

"No." She briefly rested a hand on his arm. "I like you, Jude. What woman wouldn't? You're a handsome, sexy cowboy."

To her surprise, he didn't appear particularly pleased by the compliment.

"That liking goes both ways." He spoke cautiously as if feeling his way over unfamiliar terrain. "But I think there's more between us than sexual attraction."

A chill traveled up Gabi's spine. "More?"

"Friendship for starters."

He looked sincere, even sounded sincere. But her antennae were quivering. "Friendship is all there can be."

Jude rocked back on his heels, shoved his hands into his pockets. After a moment, a boyish grin tipped his lips. "Would that friendship be served with or without benefits?"

When she didn't immediately answer, he continued, the words coming fast. "I'm open to either possibility. If you want sex to be a part of the friendship, great. If you prefer to keep it at a good-night kiss, that's fine, too. If you don't want any physical contact—" a pained look crossed his face "—I'll respect your wishes."

"That seems a bit extreme." Gabi laughed. Then, without a thought for the wisdom of her actions, she brought her mouth to his in a light kiss. "Thanks for a wonderful morning."

As she slid behind the wheel, his eyes met hers. "Are you free tonight? After the dinner with your dad?"

Jude reminded her of a tenacious terrier. The voice of reason in her head urged her not to make any commitment to see him again until she'd had time to think.

Stall. That would be the smart thing to do. She'd tell him she had plans for later tonight. She'd—

"What do you have in mind?" The question slipped past her lips before she could stop it.

His slow smile did funny things to her insides. "Do you know how to play poker?"

"I'm proficient." She quirked her lips in what her father called her Mona Lisa smile.

"Some guys and I get together once a month for Texas Hold 'Em," she heard him say. "I'd like you to fill in. Ryan's wife had a baby last week, so we're a man short."

"In case you haven't noticed—" she gazed at him through lowered lashes "—I'm a girl."

"Oh, darlin'—" Jude took off his hat and swiped his brow in an exaggerated move "—believe me, I've noticed."

Gabi laughed, as pleased by the easy camaraderie as she was flattered by the sexual overtones.

"Do you play for money?" Even as she asked, she told herself this wasn't a date they were discussing. It was simply cards. She'd been on a tight budget since coming to Horseback Hollow and could stand to pull in some extra cash.

"Fifty is the buy-in." He brushed a strand of hair back from her face. "I can front you the—"

"Not necessary."

Hope flashed in those brilliant blue eyes. "Does this mean you'll come?"

With poker on the agenda? Gabi grinned. "Wild horses couldn't keep me away."

Gabi's car had barely disappeared down the lane when Jude's mother appeared on the porch and invited him inside. Over thick slices of banana bread and strong black coffee, Jude mentioned Gabi would be filling in for Ryan tonight.

Jeanne Marie cocked her head. "I don't recall you ever inviting a woman to play before."

Jude paid close attention to the bread he was slathering with butter. "With Ryan sitting out, we're one short."

His mother topped off his coffee then resumed her seat across the table. "One of your brothers could have taken his place."

Breaking off a piece of bread, Jude shook his head. "I look at their ugly faces enough during the day."

"You like this young woman." A smile blossomed on Jeanne Marie's lips. "*Really* like her."

Denying it would be pointless. Hadn't he already declared his feelings to his family at the barbecue? He only hoped his *friend* Gabi didn't hear he loved her from one of his relatives before she was ready to accept they were meant to be together forever. "I knew Gabi was The One from the first moment I saw her."

Unlike Liam, Jeanne Marie didn't scoff. Instead her eyes turned dreamy. "It was that way between your father and me. Forty years of marriage later, we're more in love than ever."

"Gabi just wants to be friends." Jude decided he might as well lay it all out. But simply speaking the words brought back the confusion.

His mother cut her slice of banana bread precisely in half then picked up the small square, her blue eyes fixed firmly on him. "How do you feel about that?"

"It's okay." Jude shifted his gaze away, knowing his mother would be able to read the truth in his eyes. "For now."

There was no way he was telling his mother that Gabi thought he was sexy. That while all signs indicated she'd be amenable to a friends-with-benefits arrangement, she didn't appear to want more. At least not from him.

The bottom line—she'd sleep with him, but not love him. *That* was a kick in the ass.

"She's being smart." Jeanne Marie punctuated the words with a decisive nod. "The best relationships are built on a firm foundation of friendship and mutual respect. Love won't survive the ups and downs of life without a sturdy base."

Jude took a bite of bread, chewed, considered.

"You thought you were in love before," his mother gently pointed out. "Those relationships didn't last."

"This is different," he insisted. "Gabi is different."

"She very well may be." The matter-of-fact manner was as much a part of Jeanne Marie as her wide-brimmed summer gardening hats. "If she is, if what you feel for her *is* the real thing, becoming friends will only strengthen the bond between you. That's a good thing."

Jude took a drink of his rapidly cooling coffee, considered what he'd do if Gabi refused to move past the friendship stage. There was no alternative. If that happened, he'd simply find a way to change her mind.

"Honey, if the two of you are meant to be together, it will happen," his mother assured him, her voice softening. "In the meantime, inviting her to your home tonight was a smart move."

Startled, Jude inclined his head.

Jeanne Marie's smile widened. "Believe me. How a woman plays poker can tell you a lot about her."

* * *

During the drive back from Lubbock, Gabi had come to a decision. While in Horseback Hollow she'd accept Jude's friendship. "Benefits" might eventually be part of that friendship, but not until she knew Jude better and he knew her.

While a serious relationship with marriage in mind might not be possible, that didn't mean she'd cast aside her moral compass and sleep with someone she didn't know and trust. Easy-breezy, yes. But only with a healthy dose of true friendship and mutual respect tossed into the mix.

The niggling thought that Jude couldn't truly know her until she told him about the transplant was shoved aside as she considered what to wear for an evening of poker. When she played with her brothers, it was comfort clothes; yoga pants and a T-shirt. But then, she'd never cared about impressing them.

By the time the pile of clothes on her bed outnumbered those in her closet, Gabi had settled on tan pants and a royal-blue cotton sweater. Dangly earrings with brightly colored stones added a festive touch.

Since the other players were men, Gabi figured the refreshments would be salty snacks and beer. Before she left the house, she stashed a couple of bottles of water and a bag of baby carrots into her favorite grocery bag.

If the guys commented on her healthy snacks or the fact she wasn't drinking alcohol, she'd tell them she was staying sharp so she could take their money.

Her painted lips curved. The men would soon discover that wasn't far from the truth. From the time she'd been little more than a child, her analytical mind had embraced numbers and probabilities. When she reached middle school, her father reluctantly admitted he had nothing more to teach her about the game of poker. It was around that same time that her brothers began to refuse to play cards with her if money was involved.

Gabi wondered how Jude would react when he lost. Her father said you could learn a lot about a man playing cards with him, *especially* if you beat him. Which meant she was going to know Jude Fortune Jones a whole lot better by the end of the evening.

After parking in front of his home, Gabi sat for a minute. She let her gaze linger on the old farmhouse that Jude called home. The one-and-a-half-story white clapboard structure had a fresh coat of paint, a new green roof and a gorgeous wraparound porch. Half-moon pieces of stained glass over the front windows gleamed in the yard light's glow.

The warm, friendly aura emanating from the structure enveloped her when she finally stepped onto the porch and rang the bell.

When the door opened, Gabi's smile froze. Instead of Jude, his father stood in the doorway, tall and broad-shouldered in a Western shirt and jeans.

"The token female has arrived," Deke called over his shoulder, then flashed Gabi a grin and motioned her inside. "I bet you've come hoping to clean the boys and me out of our hard-earned cash."

"Ah, I guess that's the plan." Gabi roused herself from her stunned stupor. "It's good to see you again, Mr. Fortune Jones."

A pained expression skittered across his face. It was gone so quickly, Gabi wondered if she'd imagined it.

"Deke, please." He reached around her and pulled the door shut. "If you're going to make a valiant attempt to take my money, we might as well be on a first name basis."

Gabi had liked Jude's father from the moment she met him. There was no subterfuge in the man, none of the posturing so prevalent in South Beach men. Just like his son, what you saw in the rugged rancher was what you got.

"I thought I heard the door." Jude appeared in the doorway, looking positively delectable in worn jeans and a long-sleeved T-shirt the color of oatmeal. "Hey."

"Hey back at you." Gabi glanced around, taking in the ceilings with rough-sawn cedar beams, the cream-colored plastered walls and the textured rag rug on the shiny hardwood floor. On one side of the living room, plaid fabrics on wing chairs and an old deacon's bench added color and warmth. The other side of the room held a table surrounded by Windsor chairs. "You have a lovely home."

"Thank you." Jude took Gabi's hands and gave them a squeeze. His eyes never left her face. "It's good to see you."

The warmth of his gaze chased away the last remnants of the chill from the outside wind. "I'm happy to fill in."

"I was looking forward to winning some money this evening." Deke's deep voice pulled Gabi's attention back to him. "Until my son told me you're a cardsharp and I'll be lucky to have my pants when I walk out the door."

Gabi felt her cheeks pink. She shot Jude a censuring look. "I don't know where he got that idea."

"I recognized the gleam in your eyes." Jude's

teasing tone made it hard for her to hold on to her irritation. "But win or lose, you're still my girl."

Jude moved to her side, and for a second Gabi feared he meant to kiss her, right in front of his father. Instead he extended his hand. "May I take your coat?"

Feeling foolish, Gabi shrugged off the jacket. She glanced around. "Have the other players arrived?"

"Dustin and Rowdy showed up about ten minutes ago." Deke's easy manner reminded her of his son. "They're in the kitchen trying to wheedle Jeanne Marie out of another brownie."

"Your mother is here?" Gabi glanced at Jude. She thought she'd known what to expect this evening. Now she was thoroughly confused. "Is she filling in, too?"

"My parents came for dinner." Jude paused. "I'd have asked you to join us but you mentioned you had plans with your father."

"You fixed dinner for them." Gabi widened her eyes. "I'm impressed."

Deke gave a snort of laughter.

Jude shot a quick glance at his father, whose grin only widened. After placing her coat in the closet, he ushered Gabi into the living room. "My mother likes to make sure my kitchen gets some use."

Deke nudged Jude with his elbow. "What the

boy is trying to say is Jeanne Marie made the meal."

"The *boy* is a man." A muscle in Jude's jaw jumped. "And I can speak for myself."

His father only chuckled.

"Coming over and insisting on fixing a meal is something my mama would have done." Gabi's voice softened the way it always did when she thought of her mother. "She loved to putter in the kitchen."

Deke's eyes turned dark with sympathy. "I heard you lost her several years back."

"What doesn't kill you makes you stronger." Gabi forced a lightness to her tone she didn't feel, then sighed. "Or so everyone says."

"I told you she wouldn't give us another one," a male voice groused.

"She might have if you hadn't—" The dark-haired man stopped speaking when he saw Gabi. "Well, hel-lo, pretty lady."

Jude placed a proprietary hand on Gabi's arm as the two men trooped into the room, cowboy boots clicking on the hardwood.

"Dustin, Rowdy, this is Gabriella Mendoza," Jude began.

"Gabi, please," she said quickly.

"She's filling in for Ryan this evening," Jude said, then continued with the introductions.

"Pleased to meet you." Dustin, sandy-haired

with a broad smile and a baby face, pumped her hand.

Rowdy had a shock of dark hair and a gap-toothed grin. His gaze settled appreciatively on Gabi. "You're much better-looking than Ryan. If we're voting, I say he's out, you're in."

"If I take your money, you might not feel the same way," Gabi teased back.

They spent the next few minutes bonding over light banter about poker prowess. Jude had just finished explaining that his father was filling in for Liam, who'd come down with the flu, when Jeanne Marie appeared in the doorway.

"Gabriella." Jude's mother smiled broadly. "I thought that must be you at the door. You simply have to try one of my chocolate hazelnut cheesecake brownies."

Gabi hesitated.

"If she doesn't want it, can I have it?" Rowdy's question earned a scowl from Dustin, who obviously also had his eye on the sweet treat.

"She wants it." Jeanne Marie crossed the room and extended the plate holding a large chocolate square to Gabi. Though he was at least fifteen hundred miles away, Gabi swore she heard her cardiologist gasp when her gaze settled on the decadent brownie.

"My mother's brownies are legendary in this area," Jude told Gabi.

Not seeing another option, Gabi graciously accepted the treat. Before she could succumb to temptation, she broke off a bite-size piece then let Dustin and Rowdy devour the rest.

As the savory blend of chocolate, cream cheese and the faint hint of Nutella melted against her tongue, Gabi nearly moaned aloud. She found herself wishing she'd broken off a bigger piece. "That was simply heavenly."

"Won a purple ribbon at the State Fair in Dallas." Jude's mother smiled indulgently as the ranch hands once again began to pester her for more then disappeared into the kitchen when Jude announced it was time for the game to begin.

While Jude teased Gabi about not giving him any of her brownie, everyone took seats around the table. Deke picked up a deck of cards and began to shuffle. Dustin collected the money from all the players while Rowdy divvied out the brightly colored chips.

Ignoring the bowls of snack food already on the table, Gabi slipped carrots and bottles of water from her bag. When the urge to munch hit, she'd be ready. For now, her focus shifted to the cards she'd been dealt. Gabi fingered the slick surfaces and experienced a familiar thrill.

It quickly became obvious to Jude that Gabi not only knew how to play, but play well. He could tell she'd grown up around men by the easy way she teased the others at the table.

Dustin and Rowdy treated her like a sister, not a woman they'd like to date. If they had, he'd have had to make it even clearer that *his friend,* Gabriella Mendoza, was off-limits.

The final hand was dealt, and Jude stifled a low whistle when he set his gaze on his hand. *Three aces.* Smug satisfaction settled over him even as he kept his face impassive.

Rowdy dropped out first, then Dustin. His father held on a little longer before folding.

Gabi chewed her bottom lip, a clear indication she wasn't nearly as confident of the cards in her hand as she appeared. Still, with a toss of her head, she shoved all her chips into the center of the table. "I call and raise you."

It took everything Jude had to keep a grin from his lips. If she thought she could bluff a master like him, she was mistaken.

Once his chips were in the center of the table, he laid down his cards, fanning them out. "Three aces."

He started to pull in the pot, when he felt her hand on his sleeve.

"You haven't seen my cards." Her voice held cool amusement.

Dustin and Rowdy glanced at each other. Deke took a long pull of beer.

Dustin grinned. "This is going to be good."

"Show us what you got, honey," Rowdy said with a wink.

With great precision, Gabi laid out her cards. "I believe a straight beats three of a kind?"

Though she posed it as a question and her innocent expression gave nothing away, Jude wasn't fooled. He'd been taken by a master.

Dustin whooped. "It's your pot, Ga-bri-ella."

Jude cocked his head. "How long did you say you'd been playing?"

Gabi shrugged and pulled the chips to her. "Since I was, oh, eight or nine. My father says I have a knack."

"We've been snookered." Rowdy choked back a laugh before pushing his chair aside with a clatter.

Gabi looked startled when Dustin and Deke also rose to their feet. "You're leaving?"

"Gotta get a little shut-eye. Sun will be up before we know it." Dustin's gaze locked on Gabi's. "Come back and play anytime."

"It was a pleasure meeting you, Miss Gabi." Rowdy tipped his hat then shifted his gaze to Deke. "See you in the mornin', boss man."

Deke patted her on the shoulder. "It was a pleasure, little lady."

Gabi rose to her feet. "It was nice meeting you both. And seeing you again, Mr. Fortune Jo—"

She stopped at the look on his face. "Ah, Deke."

While the older man headed to the kitchen to fetch Jeanne Marie, Gabi walked the two cowboys to the door, the men in a jovial mood despite leaving with empty pockets.

Once the two cowboys were in their vehicles and she and Jude were cleaning up, he cast a sideways glance at her and made a confession. "When I saw you chewing your lip, I was certain you were bluffing."

She couldn't quite suppress a smile as she pocketed her winnings and put the chips back in the carrier.

"That was deliberate?"

Gabi laughed. "I love a good game of cards."

Was that what he'd been meant to learn this evening? That she was not only pretty, fun and sexy as hell, but possessed a mind that would constantly challenge him?

Though at the moment it was her pretty face and those full, pouty lips that called to him. He tugged her close, pleased when she melted against him. His mouth had just begun its exploration when the kitchen door swung open.

"I heard the vehicles leave—" Jeanne Marie, with her husband behind her, came to an abrupt halt in the doorway. One brow winged up.

Gabi shoved tousled hair back from her face and flushed. "I was just leaving."

Deke's gaze shifted from his wife to Gabi and Jude. "What's up?"

Ignoring her son's dark look, Jeanne Marie smiled at her husband. "I interrupted your son saying good-night to Gabi."

"Don't hurry off on our account," Deke told Gabi. "Jeanne Marie and I are heading home."

"I really have to go." Two bright dots of pink colored Gabi's cheeks.

"Don't forget this." Jeanne Marie crossed the room and lifted the market bag with a bold paisley print from the floor. "This one has to be yours. My son doesn't own anything this stylish."

During the course of the evening Jude had watched Gabi pull bottles of water and baby carrots from the brightly colored sack. Because he sensed drawing attention to her choice of snacks might bring her some good-natured ribbing from Rowdy and Dustin, he'd kept silent.

"Thank you." When Gabi slipped the now-perfectly folded bag into her purse, Jude realized she really did mean to leave before they had a chance to say good-night properly.

"Stay a little longer," Jude said in his most persuasive tone.

She may have shaken her head, but he found

himself encouraged by the regret he saw in her eyes. "I promised to have breakfast with my father tomorrow morning. That means getting up extra early."

"How is Orlando doing?" Jeanne Marie asked over her shoulder as she retrieved her and Deke's coats from the closet.

"Better." Relief skittered across Gabi's face. "The orthopedic surgeon will be stopping by tomorrow. We're hoping to learn when he'll get a walking boot."

"Once that happens—" Deke pointed a finger "—you're going to have your hands full keeping him down."

Gabi smiled. "That's a problem I'd love to have."

"I'll be in Lubbock tomorrow, both at the hospital and the rehab center," Jeanne Marie announced as she slipped on her coat. "Do you think your father would like company?"

"You're going to the hospital?" Concern sharpened Jude's voice. "Why?"

"No worries." Jeanne Marie patted her son's arm in motherly reassurance. "I'm simply filling in for Halcion. She's visiting her new grandbaby in Arizona."

Gabi inclined her head. "Halcion?"

"One of my mother's many friends," Jude responded before Jeanne Marie had a chance to open her mouth. "Hal grew up in Horseback Hollow, but moved to Lubbock several years ago."

"She and Abe volunteer at the hospital and rehab center every week," Jeanne Marie explained.

"How nice that she and her husband—"

Deke gave a snort of laughter.

"Abe is her golden retriever," Jude clarified, shooting his father a dark look.

"He's a certified therapy dog," Jeanne Marie added. "The animal has a real talent for bringing comfort to the patients."

"I've heard of therapy dogs." Interest sparked in Gabi's eyes. "But I've never seen one in action."

Jeanne Marie looped her arm through Gabi's and gave it a squeeze. "Looks like tomorrow may be your chance."

Chapter 8

As oatmeal went, the sticky substance in the bowl in front of Gabi fell into the pitiful range. The golden raisins and walnut topping, however, were excellent.

Her father looked up from his poached egg and toast. "How's your cereal?"

"Good." Gabi took a big bite, forced it down with a sip of juice when it attempted to stick. "The doctor seemed pleased by your progress."

"I'm doing *splendidly*." Orlando rolled his eyes at the word the surgeon had used more than once during his early-morning visit. "What he doesn't get is that until he gives the okay to put weight on this leg, I'm not going to be able to take care of myself."

They'd both hoped a walking boot would be prescribed, but the doctor had only said *soon*.

"Give it time, Papi. It hasn't been all that long." Even as she spoke the words, Gabi knew that to her active, vibrant father the weeks since the accident had been an eternity.

"Feels like forever." Orlando stared glumly down at his rubbery egg.

"When I spoke with Jeanne Marie last night, she mentioned coming by today." Gabi hoped the news of an unexpected visitor would lift her father's mood.

Orlando looked up, more curious than enthused. "Why?"

"Her friend, Halcion, is out of town, so Jeanne Marie is making the rounds with Hal's therapy dog."

Gabi handed the half-finished bowl of oatmeal to a nursing assistant picking up the dishes.

"Dogs come through here all the time," her father informed her. "I may know this woman's animal."

"Abe is a golden retriever."

"The dogs I've seen have all been small." Orlando stabbed the egg with his fork then looked up. "You spoke with Jeanne Marie last night? After you left here?"

"I played poker at Jude's house. Jeanne Marie and Deke were there, too," she added quickly.

Still, her father's lips pressed together. "Hadn't you already spent the better part of yesterday morning with the boy?"

The trail ride. It seemed so long ago. And it was the last thing she wanted to think about when her father's gaze was trained on her like a hawk assessing his prey.

She snatched a grape from a bowl on her father's tray and popped it into her mouth. "Jude needed a sub for poker and it sounded like fun. I cleaned them out."

Pride replaced the concern in her father's eyes. For a second he appeared to forget his worry over the time she was spending with Jude. "You surprised them."

"They didn't have a clue until it was over." Gabi discussed the hands played and how she'd won the last pot with a straight. "The weird thing is they want me back."

"They?" Orlando lifted a brow. "Or Jude?"

"Since the group only meets once a month, it's probably not going to happen. I'm sure I'll be back in Florida by the time they get together again." Gabi forged ahead, not giving her father a chance to comment. "By the way, I discovered Jeanne Marie is big on volunteering. I have to say her enthusiasm made me feel like a slug. I realized all I've done for the past couple years is work."

"You have an important job," Orlando reminded her. "It's understandable that you've focused your energies there."

Gabi couldn't argue. Her duties at the bank did keep her busy. But everyone had *some* free time. "Mom always made it a point to volunteer. I remember going with her when she delivered Meals on Wheels."

"Your mama—" a look of pride crossed his face "—she cared about people."

"I want to be that kind of person," Gabi said with a fervor that surprised her. "I've been blessed in so many ways. I want to give back."

"When you return to Miami—"

"I'm not going to wait that long, Papi." Gabi stuck out her chin. "I want to start now."

He didn't attempt to dissuade her, merely looked curious. "What do you have in mind?"

"I'm not sure yet where I want to volunteer." Gabi pulled her brows together. "But I sense an opportunity is right around the corn—"

"Is this a private conversation or may I join you?" Jeanne Marie stood in the doorway to the dining area, a huge smile on her face.

The older woman's silvery-gray hair was pulled back in a bun. Today, she wore a flowing burgundy skirt and a gauzy cotton top with burgundy splashes. Next to her a gorgeous golden retriever stood, resplendent in a red vest.

"Jeanne Marie, I'm so happy you stopped by." Gabi pushed back her chair and crossed the room to crouch by the animal. "I take it this handsome boy is Abe."

Gabi chuckled when the retriever sat and held out a paw for her to shake.

"Good-looking animal," Orlando concurred.

"You like dogs?" Jeanne Marie asked him.

"I do." Orlando straightened in his seat, his military posture reminding Gabi of all the years he'd spent in the air force. "Luz and I were both big dog lovers."

Jeanne Marie strolled to Orlando's side, the dog trotting obediently by her side. The look on the older woman's face was kind. "Luz was your wife?"

Without warning, Orlando's eyes grew misty. "Thirty-eight years we were together before God called her home."

"I can't imagine losing Deke." Jeanne Marie pulled back a chair and took a seat. The dog inched close to Orlando.

His hand dropped, and automatically he began to stroke the dog's soft golden coat. Gabi watched in amazement as the tension around her father's eyes eased.

"My husband and I have been married forty years," Jeanne Marie confided before launching into a lengthy anecdote about life in the seventies.

Gabi listened with half an ear until she heard Jeanne Marie mention her name.

"I'm enjoying this conversation so much, I wonder if you could take Abe around for me? That way your father and I can visit a little while longer."

Gabi offered a tentative smile. "I'd be happy to help. But I'm not sure of the protocol."

Jeanne Marie explained the steps, beginning with checking in at the assigned nurses' station for a list of patients open to a therapy dog visit.

"Abe is well trained," Jeanne Marie added after she finished her instructions. "Just follow his lead. And have fun."

Gabi took the dog's leash and headed down the hall toward the only nurses' station not crossed off on Jeanne Marie's list. The pleasure Gabi got at the mere thought of performing this simple act of kindness only reinforced that changes needed to be made when she returned to Miami.

Miami. The city had always been home. She liked it there. Who wouldn't? Great weather. Fabulous beaches. Not to mention an impressive nightlife. Horseback Hollow had a different feel. Warm. Homey. Of course, that could simply be because this was where her father lived now.

Still, the thought that Gabriella Mendoza might possibly be a small-town girl at heart, made her smile.

The dark-headed nurse at the circular station greeted Gabi warmly and Abe by name. She gestured down the hall toward rooms in the hospital part of the structure.

"Leslie will be transferred to the Texas Medical Center in Houston tomorrow," the RN told her. "Her parents are busy making arrangements. The girl loves animals, and I know she'd appreciate company."

The "girl" in room 202 appeared to be in her early twenties. She had muddy-brown hair cut in a chin-length bob and big blue eyes. She could have been any one of the college students Gabi saw on the streets of Lubbock except for the unhealthy yellowish tinge to her skin and fluid-filled bags under her round doll eyes. But she brightened when she saw Abe.

"Hi, Leslie. I'm Gabi. This is Abe." Gabi paused in the doorway and gestured to the retriever, whose tail swished slowly side to side. "Is it okay if we come in and visit?"

"I'd like that." The girl put down the magazine she'd been reading and smiled.

"Sucks to be in the hospital." Gabi took a seat in the chair next to the bed while Abe stood close, staring up at Leslie with his big brown eyes.

Eyes which slowly closed in doggy-bliss when Leslie began to scratch the top of his head.

"I'm being transferred to Houston tomorrow,"

Leslie told Gabi. "I've moved up on the liver transplant list, and we need to be ready."

Gabi had been too sick to remember much about the days preceding her own transplant. "That's fabulous news. Shouldn't you be out celebrating?"

The girl choked out a laugh. It died in her throat as the door opened behind Gabi.

"Jude." Pleasure lit Leslie's tired eyes.

Gabi swiveled in her seat. Her heart skipped a beat at the sight of the rugged cowboy standing in the doorway, hat in hand.

"I didn't realize you had company." Though he spoke to Leslie, his gaze remained on Gabi.

"These two are the latest." Leslie smiled at Gabi and Abe then motioned Jude inside with a hand that trembled slightly. "Delaney and Stacey were here earlier."

"My dad mentioned something about them driving to Lubbock this morning." Jude moved to pat the top of Abe's head before shooting Gabi a questioning glance.

"Your mother was having a nice conversation with my dad and she asked me to make the rounds with Abe." Gabi gestured to the girl whose now-obviously curious gaze shifted between her and Jude. "Leslie and I were just getting acquainted. How do you know each other?"

"My dad works for Jude's father," Leslie explained before Jude could respond. "He's one of the foremen."

"Bill is a stand-up guy," Jude told Gabi then turned to Leslie. "I hear you're planning a trip to Houston."

"Tomorrow," Leslie said with a weary smile.

"Big day." Jude leaned over the bed and gave the girl's hand a squeeze. "You should be resting."

"I suppose." Leslie shifted a wistful gaze to Abe. "I hope they have therapy dogs at the transplant center."

"It was nice meeting you, Leslie." Gabi rose to her feet. "I'll be thinking of you."

"Thanks." The girl shifted her gaze to Jude. "I'm glad you stopped by."

"Hey, you guys are practically family." Jude's eyes were a deep, intense blue as he gazed down at the too-thin girl. "Take care, Leslie. Good luck."

Jude followed Gabi and Abe out of the room and pulled the door shut behind him. He scrubbed a hand over his face. "You should have seen her a couple years ago. So much energy. Full of life."

"She'll be that way again." Gabi rested a hand on his arm. "They've made great strides in organ transplantation in the past decade."

"Won't she have to take all sorts of drugs?"

"I'm sure they'll be some antirejection meds

she'll have to take." Gabi kept her tone even. "It's a small price to pay for having the rest of her life."

Jude shrugged then refocused on her. "How many more patients do you have to visit?"

"Actually, Leslie was our only one on this unit." Gabi didn't bother to hide her disappointment. "We're on our way back to my dad's room now."

"I'll walk with you," Jude said.

"It was nice of you to stop by and see Leslie."

"I've known her since she was born," Jude explained. "She and my sisters used to play dolls on the front porch."

As they paused in the narrow hallway to let a gurney transporting a patient pass, Gabi reached down to stroke the dog's head.

Jude smiled. "Looks like you and Abe have bonded."

"I like dogs." Gabi let her fingers slide through the silky golden fur and felt the stirrings of regret. "Unfortunately my condo doesn't allow pets."

"You could move."

"I could. My lease is up next month." Gabi considered the possibility for a moment then shook her head. "It wouldn't be fair. I work too many hours. Dogs need someone around, at least a good share of the time."

"I grew up with dogs." Jude placed his hand

against the small of her back as they crossed the hall connecting the hospital with the rehab center. "They were never allowed in the house. My dad is old school. According to him, animals belong outside."

"As long as they have food, water and a warm place to go to when the weather turns bad, they probably love having the freedom to roam." Gabi thought of the wide-open spaces she'd seen during her ride on Sweet Betsy. "It amazes me how a person can go for miles in the countryside without seeing another soul."

Jude cast a sideways glance. "That worked in our favor yesterday."

"About that." Gabi took his arm then glanced around to make sure no one was close enough to hear. "Things got a bit out of hand."

He didn't say anything but his eyes searched hers. "I thought you enjoyed the...experience?"

"I did." Gabi lowered her voice as they strolled past a busy therapy area and tried to ignore the heat creeping up her neck. "I've been giving a lot of thought to what occurred and what comes next."

His blue eyes turned wary when she tugged him to a little alcove with two spice-colored chairs and a table topped with several current magazines. "Let's sit for a second."

Once seated, Jude stretched his long legs out

in front of him and crossed his ankles. To a casual onlooker, he'd appear relaxed, a handsome cowboy in scuffed brown boots and worn jeans. But Gabi had begun to know his face. The tight set to his jaw belied the relaxed demeanor.

She took a deep breath. "The bottom line is I can't sleep with you until I know you better," she blurted out. "Until you know me."

Something she couldn't quite identify flickered in his molten blue eyes.

"Casual sex with someone who is little more than a stranger may work for some women." She spoke quickly, fighting the urge to babble. "Not for me."

"I don't want you to consider me a stranger, Gabi." His gaze searched hers. "Not knowing each other well is an easy enough problem to fix. All we need to do is spend more time together. Unless you have plans with your father, we can start tonight."

"My dad mentioned yesterday they were having a John Wayne movie marathon tonight." Gabi laughed. "Thankfully my presence is not required."

"Perfect," Jude said. "I have something in mind you'll really like."

"What is it?"

"An event that will give you the opportunity to become better acquainted with the community and with me." He leaned over and, before she could protest, kissed her soundly. "Trust me. We won't be strangers for long."

Jude pulled up in front of Gabi's house shortly before six but didn't immediately get out of the truck. He thought about his earlier conversation with Gabi and his mother's comments about friendship being the framework of a long and happy marriage.

Tonight he and Gabi would work on building that foundation. Because he wasn't certain how long she'd be in Horseback Hollow, Jude was determined to make the most of every second with her.

The problem was he didn't feel all that upbeat tonight.

That afternoon, while moving cattle, his father had mentioned that a longtime neighbor, Roy Lerdahl—who'd been diagnosed with ALS last fall—had made the decision to sell his spread.

The land, which had been in the Lerdahl family for generations, would be auctioned off next month to the highest bidder. Jude had known Roy all his life, had gone to school with his children, apparently none of whom had an interest in ranching.

It didn't seem fair that Roy had to give up his spread. Not fair that one of the strongest—and best—men Jude knew had to face such a devastating disease.

Bad things shouldn't happen to such a good person. Anger surged, and Jude gave Gabi's door a hard punch.

"Coming." He heard her cheery voice through the thick wood.

The door opened, and Gabi stood there, a breath of fresh air and just what he needed after a hard day. She wore a flowing skirt in her trademark red and a white shirt with those little holes in it. Eyelet, his mother called it. She'd left her dark hair down, falling in gentle waves past her shoulders.

The smile on her lips faded when she saw him. "What's wrong?"

Jude whipped off his hat, raked a hand through his hair. "Crappy day."

"Come in." She took his hand, pulled him into the living room then over to the sofa, where she sat beside him. "Tell me what's wrong."

Something in her eyes said she wasn't being polite, that she really did want to know. So he told her. About growing up and seeing his father and Roy as larger-than-life. Strong, solid men who could handle anything the elements threw at them.

His disbelief when he'd heard Roy's diagnosis. And his grief and profound sadness as he watched a man he'd come to consider a friend deteriorate before his eyes. "Dad says Roy's ranch will go up for auction next month. Roy and his wife will move to an apartment in Lubbock."

"I'm sorry." Gabi leaned her head against his shoulder and her hand curled around his.

"It's just not fair." The words burst from Jude's lips like a bullet. "Roy is one of the best men I know. He doesn't deserve this."

"No, he doesn't." Sadness filled Gabi's eyes.

"Do you believe these...trials in life...are random happenings? You know, good or bad luck, or do you think there's some meaning behind them?"

"I don't have the answer." Gabi expelled a long breath. "I wish I did. When my mother was diagnosed I railed against God. How could this happen to such a good, kind, caring woman? Why not to some serial killer?"

"Exactly," Jude agreed.

"Some people say these trials in life are supposed to make you stronger." For a second Gabi's eyes took on a distant glow, then she blinked. "I say, these are lessons most of us could learn without being hit over the head and pummeled into the ground."

Jude briefly closed his eyes. "I feel so helpless. I want to help Roy but there isn't anything I can do."

"You can continue to be his friend," Gabi said softly. "You can visit him in Lubbock even when it's uncomfortable for you. Let him know he hasn't been forgotten. Sometimes when things happen, friends step away because they're not sure what to say or do. Just being there will mean a lot."

The words struck a chord in Jude's heart. "You're right. That's something I can do, something I *will* do."

"He's lucky to have you for a friend."

"Actually, he's more my dad's—"

"No," Gabi said firmly. "He's your friend, too."

"Yeah." Jude cleared the emotion from his throat. "He's my friend."

Jude slipped his arm around her shoulder, and Gabi laid her head against his chest. He pressed a kiss against her dark hair, and some of the heaviness gripping his chest lifted.

"We don't have to go out tonight," she whispered. "We can just hang out here."

"We could," he said, "but I want to show you a slice of small-town life."

"Slice of small-town life. How poetic."

He felt her smile against his shirtfront.

"Tell me, does this slice include food?" she asked. "I'm starving."

"It certainly does." He stroked her hair with the palm of his hand. "I'm taking you to an old-fashioned soup supper."

She lifted her head. "Soup supper?"

God, she was beautiful.

"All kinds of homemade soups as well as breads and desserts."

"How often are these soup suppers held?"

"Usually they have them when they need to raise money for some community cause. The one tonight is to fund a high school band trip."

Gabi straightened, shifted on the couch to face him. "Were you ever in the band?"

Had she realized that this easy conversation continued to help him relax? Or was she simply interested?

Jude shook his head. "Back then I was big into sports—football, basketball and baseball. How about you?"

"I was in the band." Her lips curved. "I attended a large high school. The band was like a big family. It gave me a real sense of belonging."

"I bet I can guess what you played." Jude cocked his head and thought for a minute. "Flute."

"What makes you think I played the flute?"

"That's what my sisters played."

"Actually I played the trumpet."

He narrowed his gaze. "You're kidding me."

"I'm not." She grinned. "My parents bought a trumpet for my brother Cisco, but he gave it up almost immediately. They didn't want to waste it, so when I told them I wanted to play an instrument, that was my only choice."

Jude pictured her with a trumpet against those full lips and felt a stirring of desire. "How'd you like it?"

"It was good." She gave a little laugh. "All my fellow trumpet players were boys."

"Sounds like you had fun in high school."

"I did," she said. "I was constantly on the run. My father was always telling me to slow down."

"Let me guess.... You didn't."

"No." A shadow crossed her face. "I didn't. What about you?"

Jude smiled. "I enjoyed high school. The sports. The parties."

"The girls," she added.

"There were a few," he admitted.

"Quite a few would be my guess."

"I imagine you had more than a few boyfriends."

"Not as many as you'd think. Four older brothers," she reminded him.

"That's right." He thought for a moment. "Of

all the guys you've dated, who was the biggest disappointment?"

When her smile faded, he wished he could pull back the question.

"There was a guy I dated in college," she said finally. "I was going through a rough period and he just…disappeared. That's why I know that Roy will appreciate your visits."

"Jerk." Jude spat the word. "If he was here, I'd punch him for you."

"Not worth it." Her gaze met his. "If I'd stayed with him, I wouldn't be here now."

He closed his hand over hers, interlocked their fingers. "Then I'm grateful."

"Is there someone I need to punch for you?" she asked with a light, teasing smile.

"I've dated lots of women," Jude admitted. "But no one who got close enough to hurt me. There wasn't anyone who captured my heart."

He brought her hand to his lips. "Until you."

Chapter 9

Though Jude had been mesmerized by Gabi
since that first intoxicating glance outside the
Superette, his feelings had begun to grow roots
and deepen. Granted, just looking at her now
brought to mind tangled sheets and sweaty
limbs. But he found the woman beneath the
beautiful and sexy exterior equally compelling.

Gabi hadn't even laughed when he told her
his surprise date was attending a soup supper
with a couple hundred of his closest friends. He
took her arm as they navigated the gravel of the
church parking lot. "In a small town, events like
these soup suppers are part of who we are and
the life we live."

"You like Horseback Hollow."

"I do." Jude glanced at the small church with its doors propped open in welcome. "I went away to college, enjoyed the clubs and nightlife then came back. This is home."

"That's how I used to feel about Miami," Gabi said with a sigh.

"Past tense?"

He slowed his pace while lifting a hand in greeting to a harried-looking couple hurrying after three towheaded boys streaking up the church steps.

"My brothers got busy with their own lives. Friends married and left Florida." Gabi expelled a ragged breath. "My mother died."

"And your father moved halfway across the country."

She nodded, bit her lip. "I was happy for him. Thrilled he'd found a job that was such a perfect fit. But—"

"You were alone."

"That was when I realized it's a close network of family and friends that gives you that warm, contented feeling, not a city." Gabi paused at the foot of the concrete steps leading up into the church then glanced down the block to the heart of the small, sleepy town. "I can see why you love it here."

"Could *you* love it here?" It was something he

needed to know. "Could you see yourself moving to a place like this?"

Gabi didn't appear to find the question strange. "I've actually given that some thought."

"And?" Though a hard knot had formed in Jude's gut, his voice remained steady.

"I believe I could," she said.

He expelled the breath he didn't realize he'd been holding. "Good."

Gabi lifted a brow.

"I'm sure your dad would like having you nearby." He gave her hand a squeeze. "I would, too."

She flushed and started up the steps. "It's not like I'm ready to quit my job and pack my bags."

"But it's a possibility," Jude said as they reached the open doors. "Down the road."

"Yes," she said. "A possibility."

Jude smiled. For now, that was good enough.

"Do you think people will find it odd we're here together?" Gabi's brows knit together in a slight frown. She stood beside Jude at the entrance to the large social hall in the church basement. "I hope they don't think we're a couple."

Jude knew that was exactly what everyone would think, and it was okay with him. "It's hard to control impressions," he said lightly, then changed the subject. "Wait until you taste the soup."

"If it tastes half as good as it smells in here, it's bound to be wonderful." She glanced around the crowded room and her eyes widened. "Look, there's Dustin and Rowdy."

The two cowboys, dressed in jeans, boots and Western-style shirts stood blatantly flirting with two young women in their twenties, one of whom Jude had dated last year.

"Are those their girlfriends?"

"I believe they're just friends." Jude smiled slightly when the brunette, Tiffany, glanced in their direction. She tossed her head and placed a hand on Dustin's arm.

Catching sight of them, Rowdy waved.

"We should say hello." Without warning, Gabi began weaving her way through the crowd. He caught up with her just as she reached the foursome.

Jude made quick work of the introductions.

Caroline, blonde and perky, asked about Gabi's father and her life in Miami.

Tiffany's cool gaze continued to shift between him and Gabi until there was a lull in the conversation.

"So." Tiff's shrewd blue eyes narrowed on Gabi. "I take it you're Jude's new flavor-of-the-day?"

Gabi's lips quirked upward. "Flavor-of-the-day?"

"Okay, maybe not the day." Tiffany's laugh held an edge. The schoolteacher slanted a glance in Jude's direction, brought a finger to her lips. "How long does it usually take for you to get tired of a current squeeze? Days? Weeks? If I remember correctly, we lasted a whole month."

When Jude scowled and shot her a warning glance, Tiffany responded with a sugary-sweet smile. He thought things were cool between them, that she appreciated him being up-front and honest when he'd felt ready to move on. Apparently he'd been wrong.

"Actually, Jude and I are simply friends," Gabi responded before he found his voice. "He's been kind enough to introduce me to the community while I'm in Horseback Hollow seeing to my father's recovery. Everyone has been extremely nice. It's easy for me to understand why my father likes living here so much."

Tiffany had the decency to look slightly abashed.

"Come on, Tiff." Caroline grabbed her friend's arm. "I want to get some of Mrs. Hansen's pasta fagioli soup before it's all gone."

"Rowdy and I'll come with you." Dustin cast an apologetic look in Jude's direction before the foursome disappeared into the crowd.

Gabi turned to Jude. Instead of jealousy, a teasing glint sparkled in her brown eyes. "Flavor-of-the-day? You never mentioned you were running an ice-cream shop of women."

"I'm not." Jude shoved his hands into his pockets. "Tiff's obviously out of sorts this evening and not making sense."

"The two of you dated."

Though it was said as a statement, not a question, Jude felt obliged to respond.

"For a short time." He rocked back on his heels. "Last fall."

"It ended badly?"

"I didn't think so," Jude said honestly. "We went out for several weeks. The initial attraction faded quickly."

"You broke up with her."

"I told her it wasn't working for me." He hadn't wanted to leave Tiff hanging, so he'd been honest. After a moment of silence, he cleared his throat. "Does it bother you?"

She met his gaze. "That you used to date her?"

He nodded.

"Not at all." She waved a hand in the air. "Why should it?"

He didn't care for the flippancy of Gabi's response or the way she appeared to take Tiffany's comments in stride. Other women would have been all over him, crazy jealous.

Maybe she simply didn't care enough to be jealous. The thought stabbed like a rusty spur.

"The flavor-of-the-day thing, though," she continued, bringing a finger to her lips. "That's intriguing."

"I don't know where she got that—"

"If you were a flavor of ice cream—" a thoughtful look crossed her face "—what would you be?"

"What's your favorite flavor?"

"Rocky Road." For a second a dreamy look filled her eyes. "I don't have it often now, but when I was younger, I could eat a big bowl of it all by myself."

"Then I'm Rocky Road." Jude wiggled his brows, a trick he'd perfected when he was thirteen and hadn't much cause to use since. "That makes me your favorite."

She laughed softly, patted his cheek. He waited for her to ask what his favorite ice cream was, but instead her gaze focused across the room on the long tables holding numerous slow cookers. "Let's check out the soups."

Squelching his disappointment, Jude strolled with her to inspect the selections.

After a few minutes of sampling and deliberation, he chose a spicy Tex-Mex chili that made his tongue sizzle. Gabi picked a sedate tomato-based soup loaded with vegetables.

While their selections were being dished up,

Jude whirled at a sudden slap on the back. The tall man with a receding hairline paused only long enough for Jude to introduce him to Gabi.

"I played football with him in high school," Jude told Gabi as his former classmate hurried off. "He's married now with four kids."

A look he couldn't decipher crossed Gabi's face.

"You need to quit slacking," she told him, sounding surprisingly serious. "Go forth and find yourself a nice woman. Settle down. Populate the earth."

"Don't worry about me. Once I go down that road, I'll make up for lost time." Jude grinned. "And have a lot of fun doing it."

Gabi took her bowl of soup from an older woman with a helmet of gray hair while Jude grabbed his from the woman's twin, then led Gabi to a nearby table.

"You want kids?" she asked in an offhand tone.

"Sure." He shrugged. "Don't you?"

She dipped her spoon into the soup. "When I was growing up, our neighborhood was filled with large families. I can remember telling my mother once that I wanted a dozen children."

"Whoa," he said.

"I don't feel that way anymore."

"Thank God." He pretended to wipe sweat off his brow.

She gave him a little smile and picked up her whole-grain roll. As he buttered his jalapeno corn bread, Jude's spirits lifted. Other than the incident with Tiff, this was turning out to be a good night.

He'd learned Gabi would consider moving to Horseback Hollow and that she wanted children. On those two matters, they were completely in sync.

At the sound of a banjo tuning up, Jude shifted in his chair toward the stage. A grizzled old man and a teenage boy were setting up. "Looks like we're in for a concert tonight. I hope you like bluegrass."

The boy took out a banjo while the white-bearded man, who Jude recognized as the boy's grandfather, pulled out a mandolin.

It wasn't long until music filled the hall. Gabi was soon tapping her foot and clapping with the rest of the crowd. When they finished their set, she cheered loudly. "They're good."

"Local talent." He nudged her elbow with his. "I bet you don't hear that kind of music much in Miami."

"Definitely not," she admitted.

The tension he'd seen on her face earlier had disappeared. Jude thought about taking her hand but held off. He might end up pushing her away with such a public display of affection. That was definitely not part of his plan.

He'd found the right woman. He was ready to settle down. And once he convinced Gabi he was the right man for her, they could live happily ever after.

Gabi strolled into the rehab center bright and early the next morning, anticipation quickening her steps. Before she left for Lubbock, she'd received a text from her father telling her he had a big surprise.

She couldn't wait to see what had him using three exclamation points. Hopefully the surprise was bigger and better than simply a decent bowl of oatmeal.

When she reached the dining room, she spotted her father at a table by the window. Gabi started to lift her hand in greeting then rushed across the room.

"When did they put that on?" she asked, gesturing to the walking boot.

"The doctor came by at the crack of dawn and gave the okay." Orlando's smile flashed then disappeared. "It hurts like a—" He paused, appeared to consider his words. "It's very uncomfortable when I put weight on the foot."

"The therapist is going to work with him later

today on using a platform walker." Obviously overhearing the conversation, Carla, her father's pretty, red-haired primary nurse, stopped beside the table.

Gabi had spoken with Carla many times about her father's progress, and she'd always been helpful. The RN never acted as if her questions were an imposition. In fact, several times their conversations had ventured into the personal realm. Gabi knew Carla had grown up in Horseback Hollow and still lived there, commuting every day to her job in Lubbock.

"Won't using a walker be hard with his broken arm?" Gabi kept her tone offhand, not wanting to worry her father.

"It's more difficult," the nurse agreed, then smiled at Orlando. "But the type of walker the doctor has prescribed is designed specifically for a person in his situation."

Gabi glanced at her father then back at Carla. "That's good news."

She found the nurse staring. "Didn't I see you last night at the soup supper? You were there with Jude Fortune Jones."

Out of the corner of her eye, Gabi saw her father lower the cup of coffee and fix his gaze on her.

Busted.

Gabi nodded, smiled brightly. "Wasn't the

soup spectacular? And I loved the entertain-
ment."

"That was my grandpa and brother." The
nurse turned toward Orlando. "Bluegrass music.
Derek plays the banjo and my grandfather is a
whiz on the mandolin."

"I'm sorry I missed it." Orlando sipped his
coffee, the look in his eyes telling Gabi once
they were alone she had some explaining to do.

The phone in the nurse's pocket buzzed. She
pulled it out and glanced at the readout. "I'll be
back in a few minutes with your medications."

"No hurry." Orlando waved a dismissive hand.
"My daughter and I have a few things to discuss."

The minute the nurse was out of earshot, her
father met her gaze. "You were with him again."

His tone was as flat as his eyes.

"It was a fundraiser for a high school band
trip." Gabi could have cheered when her voice
came out casual and offhand, just as she'd intended. "Soup, bread and desserts. All for a five-
dollar donation."

"I don't have a problem with you supporting
local youth groups," Orlando said pointedly. "I
do have an issue with you spending every free
moment with that cowboy."

"I don't see why." Gabi pressed down her irritation. "Jude is a nice guy from a well-respected family."

"He's using you."

"As we haven't had sex, I don't see how."

Orlando winced. "Gabriella."

"Let's call a spade a spade, Papi. You think all Jude wants is to get me into bed, and obviously you believe I'm so weak I'll do it just because he pays me a few compliments."

"Mija—"

"That attitude is as insulting to me as it is to him." Gabi lifted her chin.

"You forget, I raised four boys. I know what men—"

"You also raised one daughter. One who makes her own decisions."

"I know—"

"Apparently you don't or there wouldn't be a reason to have this discussion." Gabi took a deep breath and reminded herself she'd made her point. There was no need to beat it into the ground.

Seeing the distress on her father's face, her anger dissipated. She placed a gentle hand on his arm. "I can take care of myself. Don't worry about me."

Orlando smiled. "Asking a father not to worry about his little girl is like asking the sun not to rise in the morning."

"Please. Try." Gabi bent over, kissed his cheek. "I'll stay for your therapy this morning then I'm heading back to Horseback Hollow."

Orlando opened his mouth. Shut it.

"Not to see Jude," she said, answering his unspoken question. "To speak with Jeanne Marie and find out where I can put my talents to work in the community."

Jude spent the better part of the morning helping his father put out hay for the cattle and inspect the property's perimeter. When he returned to the house for some fencing, his heart stopped at the sight of Gabi's car in the driveway.

Though Gabi had appeared to enjoy his company at the soup supper, when he'd tried to set up another date, she'd been evasive. Which didn't make sense, considering their earlier discussion.

Still, he'd been encouraged by the heat of the kiss they'd shared as well as the progress they'd made in getting better acquainted.

Jude glanced down at his jeans. Though his mother didn't like dusty work clothes in her parlor, this time it couldn't be helped. Still, he stomped off most of the dirt from his shoes and swatted his pants with his hat before stepping inside.

The second he opened the front door, Jude heard the sound of feminine laughter. He stuck his head around the corner. "You're having a party and didn't invite me?"

Jeanne Marie chuckled. "You're always welcome, honey. Is your daddy with you?"

Jude shook his head. "He's still out."

"Well, come and sit down. We're having tea and cream puffs."

His mother might be having cream puffs. The one on the tiny plate in front of Gabi had barely been touched. But then Jude had noticed his future wife wasn't much for sweets.

"It's nice to see you again, Miss Mendoza." Jude flashed a smile and, despite his polite words, took a seat right next to her on the sofa.

"My goodness, Jude, give the girl some room. There's plenty of space on that sofa."

Winking at Gabi, Jude made a great show of scooting over…just a little.

"Would you like a cream—" his mother began.

"This will work." Lifting the one off Gabi's plate, he took a big bite then had to reach for a napkin as the filling exploded.

"I declare, Gabi's going to think you were raised by wolves." His mother slapped at his sleeve. "That was hers."

"I don't mind, Jeanne Marie." Gabi sounded as if she was trying to swallow a laugh. "While the cream puff is delicious, one bite was perfect."

"If you decide you'd like another one, let me know." Jeanne Marie shot Jude a narrowed, glinting glance. "Later, you and I will have a talk about manners."

Jude offered his mother a conciliatory smile. "Don't let me interrupt your conversation."

"You already have," his mother said with an exasperated sigh, then lifted her teacup and studied Gabi over the rim. "Do any of the volunteer opportunities we've discussed interest you?"

Gabi's expression turned thoughtful. Jude thought she looked especially pretty today in a bright yellow sweater the color of the sun.

Then there were those gorgeous eyes—large, dark brown and full of secrets. Jude could stare at her all day. But not with his mother gazing at him, a bemused look on her lips.

"I'd like to do something with Texas No-Kill," Gabi said after a long moment. "Do what I can to solicit more foster families for the animals."

Jude decided his mother must have told Gabi how the no-kill animal shelter, located between Horseback Hollow and Vicker's Corners, had been struggling. Delbert Knolls, the volunteer director, had recently left the organization because of declining health.

"How do you propose to do that?" Jude asked.

"I haven't seen the place. Or spoken with the people involved with it." Gabi lifted a shoulder in a slight shrug. "Until I have, it'd be presumptuous of me to offer any suggestions."

Beautiful and smart, Jude thought.

"I can introduce you to Steve Watkins," he told her. "He's a local banker who has temporarily taken the reins of the shelter until someone agrees to manage it permanently."

"That's sweet of you, Jude." Jeanne Marie beamed at her son. "I didn't realize you were interested in volunteer work."

"On the contrary." Jude shifted his gaze and fixed it on Gabi. "I'm very interested."

Chapter 10

Gabi strolled with Jude toward the café where they would meet the acting director of the no-kill animal shelter. She tried to stay focused on the upcoming meeting, but her thoughts kept drifting to the handsome man beside her.

Jude's dark blond hair gleamed in the streetlight's glow. Since the afternoon, he'd showered, shaved and splashed on cologne; a subtle enticing scent that tempted her to lean close. Tonight he wasn't wearing his trademark Stetson or his Tony Lama boots. A darn shame because she found the cowboy look appealing.

But he looked sexy as sin in dark pants and a black sweater. A far cry from the dusty jeans and muddy boots he'd worn into Jeanne Marie's parlor.

He'd certainly earned his mother's wrath for coming into the house in his work clothes. Though Jeanne Marie hadn't said anything with "company" present, Gabi had overheard the older woman's sharp words to her son when she'd slipped back into the house to retrieve the purse she'd forgotten.

Jeanne Marie's terse comments reminded Gabi of her mother's futile attempts to civilize her four brothers. It often seemed to her as if the boys acted up just to see Luz's fiery temper flare. Gabi's lips curved. Unless you'd been the one on the receiving end of her mother's temper, the show had always been entertaining....

"Something funny?"

"I was thinking of my mother." Gabi's smile inched wider. "My brothers were always pushing her buttons. I really believe they enjoyed getting her riled up."

"Probably." Something in his grin told her he and his brothers had done the same. "I suppose you were a little angel."

"Always."

"I have a thing for angels." Jude slung an arm around her shoulder. "Especially those fluffy wings. So sexy. Perhaps you can show me yours…later?"

A giggle bubbled out from Gabi's throat. Though *giggling* wasn't something she'd done since high school, it fit her upbeat mood. If they weren't on a public street, she'd plant a big kiss right on Jude's mouth just, well, because she was so happy. Being here. With him.

But kissing Jude on Horseback Hollow's Main Street in full view of the citizenry wouldn't be wise. Gabi took a deep breath, forcing her eyes—and her thoughts—from his mouth. "Tell me about Mr. Watkins."

Thankfully, Jude didn't seem to find the question odd.

"His family owns several banks in the area." His hand slid down to link fingers with her.

Gabi wished they could keep on walking, just the two of them. Talk and laugh and get to know each other better under the light of a full moon. But they had a meeting to attend. One she'd requested. "Has he always been interested in animal welfare?"

"You can ask Steve yourself." Jude gestured with one hand. "That's him now, getting out of the BMW roadster."

"Looks like we're both early." The stocky man lifted a hand in greeting. He had stylishly cut short dark hair and direct hazel eyes. Several inches shorter than Jude, he carried himself with a quiet confidence. He extended a hand. "Steve Watkins. You must be Gabriella."

His handshake was firm, his gaze admiring.

"It's a pleasure to meet you." Gabi pretended not to notice he held her hand several seconds longer than necessary. "Please, call me Gabi."

"I'm sorry about what happened to your father." Steve cast a sideways glance at Jude. "Are they still thinking the accident may be retaliation against the Fortunes?"

"Possibly." Although Jude's back stiffened, his tone remained even. "According to Sawyer, we won't know if there was tampering with the landing gear until the NTSB finishes their investigation."

Steve shifted his attention back to Gabi. "How's your father?"

"He's making solid progress," she told him. "He got a walking boot today,"

"That's good news." Steve opened the door to the café then stepped back to let Gabi pass. "My brother had to wear one of those boots after he fractured his ankle last year. It took him a while to adjust, but it made a big difference in his mobility."

The waitress led them to a corner table. As soon as they ordered, Steve began to pump Gabi for personal information. When he discovered she was in the banking industry, he positively beamed.

"You can have your cattle and horses, Jude." Steve shot Gabi a conspiratorial smile. "This woman and I know the thrill that comes from seeing a spike in closed-end agreements."

A muscle in Jude's jaw jumped. "There's a lot more to running a successful ranch than tending livestock."

"Of course," Steve said dismissively then refocused on Gabi. "So you're interested in volunteering at the animal shelter."

"I am. But I'm only here until my father is back on his feet." Gabi wanted to be completely up-front. "The way he's progressing, that might not be very much longer."

Talk of the shelter filled the conversation while she ate her salad and the men chowed down on burgers. Steve explained the challenges faced by the no-kill shelter. Jude not only provided history on the shelter's early days from information gleaned from his parents, but indicated he had an interest in volunteering.

"I hate to cut this short but I have a board meeting tonight." Steve leaned forward, closing the distance across the table between him and Gabi. "I'm free tomorrow. We could grab something to eat, discuss the various volunteer jobs in more depth once you've had a chance to think about them overnight."

"Gabi and I have dinner plans tomorrow," Jude answered before she could respond. "But we would be available later in the evening."

Steve inclined his head slightly at Jude's emphasis on *we*.

"Gabi and I are dating," Jude confirmed, dipping a French fry into a mound of ketchup. "We're practically going steady."

Gabi dropped her fork to her plate with a clatter.

Steve only laughed. "Message received loud and clear."

"Eight o'clock work for you?" Jude asked Gabi.

Gabi merely smiled and gave a jerky nod.

"It's a plan." Steve's phone gave a little beep. He glanced at the readout and grimaced. "Sorry. I need to head out."

When they reached the sidewalk, Steve paused, focused those hazel eyes on Gabi. "We're always looking for qualified people for management positions in our banks. If you decide to stay in this area, I'd be interested in discussing various opportunities we might have for you."

"Thank you," she said. "I'll keep that in mind."

"That went well." Jude reached around her to open the truck door.

"Which part? The part where you told Steve we had plans for tomorrow night when we didn't? Or when you took a time machine back fifty years and said we were *going steady?*" She paused for a breath, not certain if she should be irritated or flattered. "Or perhaps you're referring to when you decided to volunteer so I won't be alone with him?"

"I'm not sure what you mean." Jude's innocent expression didn't fool her in the least. "Hearing you and Steve talk, I was seized with the volunteer spirit."

"Let me make one thing clear." Her gaze met his. "If I wanted to meet with Steve alone, if I wanted to go out with him, I would."

His smile turned sheepish. "I guess I overstepped."

"By about a mile."

He took a deep breath, let it out slowly. "I'm sorry, Gabi."

"Apology accepted." Impulsively, she looped her arm through his. "Yet, I have to say I'm glad you volunteered."

Startled surprise crossed his face. "You are?"

"Certainly." Gabi gazed up at him through lowered lashes. "Volunteers are always needed to clean cages."

"Remind me again why you're cooking tonight," Gabi asked, munching on a piece of celery. "And why it had to be at my dad's place instead of your own?"

"A change of scene is always good." He took a sip of the sparkling grape juice he'd brought with him and continued to stir the contents of the bowl in front of him. "Besides, if I made dinner at my place, the stove might convulse at being used twice in one week."

Gabi laughed. "We could have gone out."

"I'm more than capable of preparing a meal," he said, then winked. "For my steady girl."

"Until I'm wearing your class ring on a chain around my neck—" she leaned over and kissed him "—we're not going steady."

The look of pleasure on his face made her smile.

"What are you making?" She moved to the counter by the stove, where he was blending a baking mix with some milk. On the stove ground beef, onion and four cans of vegetables had just come to a boil.

"Dumplings." He swatted her hand away when she reached for the mixing spoon. "Every bit as good as Martha Stewart's."

While she watched, he spooned the mixture over the stew, then reduced the heat and covered the pot.

"Should be done in twenty."

Jude looked so proud of himself that Gabi took a step forward and slid her arms around his waist. "You're quite a guy, Jude."

"Took you a while to notice."

"Oh, I noticed right away." She gazed up at him. "What I didn't expect was that you'd continue to impress me."

"Oh, darlin', I'm just getting started." His head jerked up. "Perfect. They're playing our song."

Gabi cocked her head and listened intently. Jude had brought his iPad with him. Before he'd started dinner, they'd enjoyed a glass of sparkling grape juice while music from his playlist created a warm, intimate atmosphere in the living room.

But from where she stood in the kitchen, she couldn't hear the tune now playing. "What song is it?"

"Hold on." Jude dashed from the room and a second later the melodious tones of Adele could be clearly heard.

"It's our song," he said with satisfaction when he strolled back into the kitchen.

Gabi recognized the artist but not the tune. "Does 'our song' have a title?"

"'Crazy for You.'" Jude held out his hands. "May I have this dance?"

"You're crazy."

"I'm crazy...for you." His arms were strong and sure as he maneuvered her into the living room, where the coffee table had been mysteriously moved to the side, creating a small dance space in the center of the room.

Resting her head against his broad chest, cosseted in his arms, Gabi felt as if she could face anything…as long as Jude was with her.

As they swayed to the bluesy melody, she let the world and any worries slip away. When "their" song ended, an equally romantic one took its place.

"Do your brothers know you have Neil Sedaka on your playlist?" Gabi tilted her head back to meet his gaze.

Jude winced.

"It'll be our secret," she whispered loudly, and he grinned.

His arms tightened around her. "I'm glad you let me come over tonight."

She lifted a brow. "Did I have a choice?"

"You always have a choice." Jude's lips brushed her hair. "To leave. To stay."

Gabi's heart wrenched. If only that were true. The transplant had given her life, but had taken some choices out of her hands. Her relationship with Jude would have to stay casual. It wouldn't be fair for her to pursue a future with him while having such an uncertain future. But for tonight she was going to pretend she was a twenty-five-year-old woman with her life stretched out before her and not a care in the world.

"We dance as if we've been doing it our whole lives," he murmured.

"For a guy who breaks horses and herds cattle, you're surprisingly light on your feet."

"My grandmother loved ballroom dancing." The deep voice against her ear sent a shiver of desire coursing up her spine. "She passed that love on to my mother. My dad isn't the dancing type. So when we got old enough—"

"Jeanne Marie taught you to dance."

He chuckled and looked faintly embarrassed. "Let's just say she tried her best."

"You know how I told you my father taught me the ins and outs of poker?" With a laugh she shook her head. "What I didn't tell you was Mama didn't like that one bit."

Gabi's mother had been a definite force to be reckoned with in their household. Luz Mendoza had been a fiery, determined woman with a big heart.

"You miss her." Jude's soft voice encouraged confidences.

Initially prepared to change the subject, Gabi reminded herself—again—that talking about things that mattered was the only way she and Jude would get to know each other.

"She was my best friend," Gabi said simply, meeting his gaze. "I could go to her with my worries and know she'd understand. We were two women surrounded by a sea of testosterone."

His eyes searched hers as they swayed to a Michael Bublé classic. "How did she die?"

"Cancer." The word was bitter on her tongue. "We had time to say our goodbyes. I guess that was something...."

His hand tightened on hers. "I'm sorry."

"Yeah, me, too." Gabi fought the dark cloud trying to settle over her by reminding herself she'd been lucky to have such a mother. Not to mention a very happy childhood.

Until my freshman year in college. An unexpected chill stole over her and she shivered.

"Don't tell me you're cold." He rubbed his hands up and down her arms.

The ding from the stove made any response unnecessary.

"I've wowed you with my dancing prowess." Jude tugged her to the already-set table. "Now prepare to be impressed by my superb culinary skills."

A half hour later, Gabi had to admit that Jude's "Rush Hour Stew" was delicious. Best of all, the no-salt-added vegetables fulfilled her daily vitamin requirements.

"I didn't think about dessert," he admitted.

"That's okay." She took a sip of the ice-cold

skim milk she'd chosen to drink with her meal. "I'm not much for sweets."

"I've noticed." Jude smiled lazily. "You're extremely health conscious."

He'd given her the perfect opportunity to tell him about her transplant. They were alone, relaxed, and there was plenty of time before their meeting with Steve. Gabi wasn't sure why she'd held back the information. After all, it couldn't remain a secret forever. "I believe in taking care of my body. I—"

Her phone rang. She stifled a curse.

"Ignore it," Jude urged.

"I can't." She pushed up from the table and retrieved her cell phone from the counter. "It might be the rehab center."

She glanced at the unfamiliar number on the readout and her stomach contracted.

"This is Gabriella Mendoza." She listened for a moment and felt the knot in her stomach melt away. "No. I don't mind. I can stop by the shelter tomorrow and speak with the supervisor."

"Who was it?" Jude asked when she slipped the phone into her pocket.

"Steve." Gabi shrugged. "Tonight's meeting is off. Something came up."

"You don't seem upset."

"That's because I'm not. Now we don't have to rush off to meet with him." Gabi glanced at the table and the sink filled with dirty dishes. "Since you cooked, I'll clean up."

"Hold off for a minute." Jude sprang to his feet and held out a hand. "Since we have time, sit on the sofa with me. Take a few minutes to relax."

"Relax?" His innocent expression didn't fool her a bit. "You want to just…relax?"

Jude held up his hands, palms out. "If you find me irresistible and choose to kiss me, well, that's your choice."

Gabi laughed and shook her head. The guy was likable. Not to mention…irresistible.

For that reason alone she should package up the last of the stew and send him on his way. But the second the thought of fleeing crossed her mind, she squelched it. Wasn't this closeness what she'd wanted? Hadn't she told him they had to be friends before she could sleep with him?

Now that she found herself flooded with feelings of…friendship, sending him away made no sense at all. "Let me at least clear the table. Then we can relax."

To her surprise, Jude pitched in without being asked. It was another positive factoid to add to her growing Jude Fortune Jones book of knowledge. "You'll make some woman a good husband."

"Glad to know I've impressed you again," he said, an engaging twinkle in his eyes.

"Since I'll be leaving town shortly, if any woman needs someone to vouch for your positive attributes, you can give them my number." The simple realization that the woman who would one day capture Jude's heart wouldn't be her brought a sharp, slicing pain.

"I appreciate the offer, darlin'—" The words flowed easily from his lips. "But I'm not looking at other women."

"Maybe not right now," she said lightly. "But you will be eventually."

His eyes met hers and Gabi's heart gave three hard thumps.

Jude opened his mouth, closed it without speaking then drew her to the sofa. When they were settled, he looped an arm around Gabi's shoulder, his gaze focused on her mouth. "I have a question for you."

"Yes." She flashed a smile. "You may now kiss me."

"Ah, great, but that wasn't my question." The normally confident cowboy looked oddly flustered. "Friday is Valentine's Day."

"Really?" The knowledge made her feel slightly ill. When she'd taken her leave from the bank, she'd calculated that between vacation and sick days she had enough time built up to take her to the middle of February. Which meant she'd receive one more paycheck before the money stopped....

"Do you have plans?"

"Pardon?"

"Plans. Do you have plans for dinner on Valentine's Day?"

"I hadn't given it much thought." Gabi gave a little laugh. "I'll probably do something really romantic, like pig out with my dad on red Jell-O in the rehab dining room, then come home and go to bed. What about you?"

"While your current plan sounds like tons of fun, I have an alternative suggestion." He toyed with a piece of her hair, sliding the silky strands between his fingers. "Though it's hard to compete with Jell-O."

"Almost impossible," she conceded, a smile hovering at the corners of her lips. "Cherry is my absolute favorite."

"There's a new restaurant in Vicker's Corners," Jude said casually. "They have a diverse menu, so you should be able to find something you like, though I doubt red Jell-O is on the menu."

They exchanged a smile.

"There's a small dance floor," he continued in a persuasive tone, "which would give us a chance to show off the moves we perfected this evening."

Gabi tried to ignore the heavy pounding of her heart. In her mind, she'd always thought of Valentine's Day as a special day—one for couples in love, or who were thinking about being in love. Perhaps she should add couples considering *making love* to the list. Regardless, she found herself oddly touched by the offer. "Are you asking me out on a real date, Mr. Fortune Jones?"

"We've been on dates before." He lifted a fist, counting off the events by raising a finger. "The barbecue."

"That wasn't a date," she scoffed. "That was the night we were introduced."

He simply smiled and continued. "The trail ride. The poker game. The soup supper. After tonight's meal, I'll have to move to my other hand."

"Those weren't dates," she argued.

"Semantics." Jude's fingers closed around hers. "Say you'll come. You know we'll have a great time. We always do."

Gabi brought a finger to her lips. "I'd need to speak with my dad first to make sure he hasn't made any plans that involve me. Since I can't say yes right now, if you want to ask someone else—"

"There isn't anyone but you." He trailed a finger down her cheek, his blue eyes focused intently on her.

Gabi's breath caught in her throat.

"I want you," he said in a soft, low tone as his hand slid over hers, engulfing it with gentle pressure. He planted a kiss to the side of her lips, his mouth warm against her skin. "Only you."

His arms were around her, clasping her against a wall of muscle before he focused on scattering little love bites along her jaw. "The fact that you're always so covered drives me wild."

She laid her lips against his cheek, found the slightly rough texture arousing. "Oh, Jude."

His fingers raked through her hair, and his lips pressed to hers in an intoxicatingly sweet kiss that seemed to last forever. Yet, not nearly long enough.

She wrapped her arms around his shoulders, wanting the closeness, the connection, to continue.

As if he understood, Jude took it slow, his mouth moving from her lips then back again in unhurried caresses that only stoked the fire flowing through her veins.

His hands roamed then lingered over her breasts, his fingers teasing her nipples to points through the thin cotton of her shirt and bra.

Gabi's breath quickened as the kisses and touching continued—soft, urgent, relentless. Her control became a thin thread stretched further by each kiss, each touch, each caress. When his tongue swept her lips and slipped inside, the last strand snapped.

A moan escaped her lips. A desperate ache rose low in her belly. She pressed against him, offering herself to him, wanting him to give her the same pleasure he'd given her by the pond.

She gasped in protest when he pulled back without warning and strode to the window. Gabi watched in stunned disbelief as he pushed back the curtains and stared out into the darkness, his hands braced on the windowsill.

Gabi would have moved to him, but her trembling knees wouldn't support her. "What's wrong?"

He turned, his eyes dark.

"I want you, Gabi. I've never wanted anyone more." Jude rubbed his neck and scowled. "But not here. Not in your father's house. I can't make love to his daughter under his roof while he's in the hospital."

She supposed she could have denied they were on the verge of making love, told him there was nothing wrong with kissing on the living room sofa. But the raw need that still held her in its grip told a different story.

So Gabi didn't argue. She let him take her

hand and even gave him one quick kiss before he walked out the door. The ache she felt when he got in his truck and drove off was only a prelude, she realized, to the devastation she would feel when he walked out of her life for good.

Chapter 11

After receiving her father's reluctant blessing and leaving the rehab center at two, Gabi spent the rest of Friday afternoon getting ready for her date with Jude. It had been a long time since she'd indulged herself, so she took a long bath then brought out her favorite pear-scented lotion. She smoothed it over her body, the pads of her fingers tracing the raised scar than ran down the front of her chest, between her breasts.

My battle scar, she thought to herself, then sent up a prayer of thanks to the young man who'd died and whose family had generously donated his organs.

The heart that now beat strong and sure had been a great gift, one she didn't take for granted.

Though she knew the scar wasn't pretty, she still didn't understand the horrified looks on the faces of those at the pool party, and the memory still stung every time she caught her reflection.

Their reaction made her wonder what Jude would think when he saw it. Would he be shocked? Disgusted? Or would he view the scar as she did, as a symbol of a life-giving act?

She didn't need to worry about that now, because she didn't plan on letting him see it. Not yet. Perhaps never. Even if things went as she anticipated tonight and they made love, she could hide it by insisting the room be dark. If he felt the ridges of the scar on her skin, she'd simply tell him she had heart surgery. In a few weeks, she'd return to Miami and her life there.

Instead of excitement, the thought of leaving made her sad. She liked Horseback Hollow. The people were friendly and the pace suited her. She wished she could be here when the flowers were in bloom and the leaves had sprouted on the trees.

Gabi imagined herself attending parties, barbecues and picnics. It wouldn't be long before she knew everyone in town and they knew her.

If she and her father were in the same town, she could meet him for lunch, or invite him over for the evening. She and Jude...

Like a movie in slow motion, images played

in her mind. She and Jude riding horses across windblown pastures, swaying to romantic songs with melodies that wrapped around them like a pretty ribbon, walking down Main Street with fingers entwined…

Stop, she told herself, *stop the madness.*

For too many reasons to count there could be no her and Jude. Whatever was between them was transient. Which made the possibility of her staying in Horseback Hollow simply wishful thinking.

If Gabi made the small Texas town her home, she'd have to sit back while Jude met another woman, fell in love and raised children. Despite wanting what was best for him, she couldn't bear to watch the man she loved build a life with someone else.

Man she *loved?*

Gabi's heart stuttered. She couldn't be in love with Jude. Love took time to develop—months, often years.

She respected Jude, admired his caring, compassionate nature and enjoyed spending time with him. She…

Gabi sighed. What was the point in lying to herself? She loved him. But the fact that he now had her heart changed nothing. The doctor had warned her it wouldn't be wise for her to bear children. Nor could she guarantee, despite her best efforts, she'd stay healthy. Heck, she couldn't guarantee she'd be around to celebrate a single anniversary.

She knew her father believed she should tell Jude about the transplant. But the way she viewed the situation, it didn't make sense to put a damper on their impending fling with all the heavy medical talk and questions that were bound to ensue. And Gabi certainly didn't want Jude to begin treating her with kid gloves, as if she was fragile.

Still, she didn't like keeping this from him....

When sadness tried to gain a foothold, Gabi firmly reminded herself this was a day for love and romance. Though she might not be able to profess her love, she could show Jude how she felt. Tonight, if everything went as anticipated... she'd give him her body as she'd given him her heart.

Her lips quirked upward. Before she took off her clothes, she had to put some on. Since she hadn't been sure how dressy the café would be, Gabi had checked the internet. Thankfully, the management of The Garden appeared firmly grounded in the twenty-first century. She found pictures—both interior and exterior—and a menu online.

The only comparison between this place and The Horseback Hollow Grill appeared to be that they were both eating establishments in the state of Texas.

The place looked decidedly upscale, so Gabi decided on a red lace dress with the high neckline she'd purchased in an after-Christmas sale. Expert use of the curling iron turned her normally wavy hair into a mass of tumbled curls. Lipstick, the same shade as her dress, was carefully applied.

Gabi was happy she'd gone to the extra effort when she opened the door and saw Jude. The man looked positively scrumptious in a suit, a crisp white shirt open at the neck and sleek black oxfords.

"These are for you." He offered her a florist's box tied with a white ribbon with silver threads.

When she opened it, Gabi found two dozen red roses nestled inside. Their fragrant scent filled the room.

"They're lovely." Gabi swallowed past the lump in her throat. "Thank you. Let me put them in water."

She quickly arranged the flowers in a cut-crystal vase and gave them one last look before she got into his truck and they drove to Vicker's Corners.

Jude laughed when Gabi mimed her dad's reaction to the rehab center's plans to show a romantic comedy in the lounge that evening.

"The male patients threatened to boycott," Gabi informed Jude.

He turned off the highway toward Vicker's Corners. "Were their demands met?"

"They most certainly were." Gabi grinned. "The very romantic *Live Free or Die Hard* will now be on the screen this evening."

Jude chuckled and slowed when they reached the town's quaint business district. The sidewalks were filled with couples enjoying the warm evening. "I'll drop you off at the café then look for a parking space."

"Absolutely not." Gabi's tone brooked no argument. "It's a beautiful evening. I'd enjoy a stroll."

He stopped the truck and waited for a car to back out of a parking spot. "Are you certain you'll be okay walking several blocks?"

She gave him a long, penetrating look.

Turning the wheel sharply, he commandeered the vacated space and grinned. "Message received loud and clear."

"I've been walking in heels most of my life," Gabi said when he helped her out of the truck, pleased when she saw his gaze linger on her legs.

The look he shot her three-inch heels was clearly disbelieving.

"I could run a marathon in these shoes," she insisted.

"I'm not saying a word." Jude smiled, a boyish sort of smile that sent her stomach into flips and melted her heart.

The antique streetlights were on, lending a golden glow to the night. Laughter and what sounded like a mix between rock and country music spilled out to the street from several drinking establishments.

"I heard on the radio the area hit record highs today," Gabi said conversationally as they walked down the street.

"A perfect evening." He leaned over and kissed her cheek. "With the perfect woman."

Gabi laughed self-consciously. "I'm hardly perfect."

"C'mon." He put a hand protectively around her waist when they were forced to navigate through a crowd of casually dressed couples on the sidewalk outside a Tex-Mex cantina. "You even eat right."

"That's something everyone should do," she pointed out.

"I try," Jude admitted. "But it's my fondness for sweets that gets me in trouble. My mother had to put a padlock on the cookie jar when I was growing up."

Gabi shot him a look telling him she knew full well that was a gross exaggeration. She'd been around him enough to see that while he liked desserts, he didn't overindulge.

"I read somewhere once that you get one hundred percent satisfaction from the first bite of something." Gabi kept her tone casual, hoping she didn't sound as though she was preaching. "When I'm tempted to eat too much I tell myself one bite is all I need. A bonus is fewer calories and minimal artery-clogging fat."

His gaze slid sideways. "You certainly don't have to worry about extra weight."

"Best to be proactive." Then, realizing how prim that sounded, she flashed a smile. "I bet you're sorry now that you didn't bring me candy. I'd have one bite and the rest would have been yours."

Jude snapped his fingers, shook his head. "Blew that one."

They exchanged a smile. Time seemed to stretch and extend. He took her hand. It was as if they were two young lovers out for an evening stroll without a care in the world.

"That wasn't even two blocks." A hint of regret filled her voice when the elaborate hand-painted sign came into view.

The Garden sat smack in the middle of a block of cute little shops. Couples dressed for a special evening lingered on the outside sidewalk. Gabi wondered if they'd have to wait, but when Jude gave the hostess his name, they were immediately escorted to a table.

"The power of a reservation," Jude quipped as he pulled out her chair with a flourish. The small zebrawood table by the window was adorned with a bud vase holding a deep red rose and sprigs of baby's breath.

"This is very nice." Gabi let her eyes linger on the interior of the trendy bistro. She admired the stained glass windows, the copper ceiling tiles and vintage Art Nouveau French crystal chandelier in the entryway.

She pulled her gaze from the cut-glass crystals. "I'm surprised you were able to get a reservation here on such short notice."

"Actually I called several weeks ago, not long after we first met." He took a seat opposite her. "I figured if you didn't want to come here, I'd cancel."

She picked up the menu. "Or ask someone else."

"Why would I do that? The only woman I want to spend time with is you." He appeared genuinely perplexed.

She started to chuckle, then realized he was serious. The knowledge alternately pleased and terrified her.

"Well, I appreciate the invitation." She politely took the wine list the waiter handed her, though she had no intention of drinking. "Especially since I discovered *green* Jell-O was on the rehab center menu tonight, not red."

"Yes, but they are showing *Live Free or Die Hard.*"

"Sacrifices had to be made." Gabi tried to stay serious but ended up making a face, drawing a laugh from him.

Jude reached over and took her hand. "Seriously, thank you for spending the evening with me."

She lost herself in his clear blue eyes. Finally, reluctantly, she slipped her hand from his and focused on the menu. "What's good here?"

"From what I've heard—" Jude opened his menu "—you can't go wrong with anything on the menu."

After some serious flip-flopping—because everything sounded enticing—Jude ordered a steak and Gabi selected the teriyaki salmon.

The waiter took their menus then discreetly returned several minutes later with their drinks. As Gabi smiled at the server, her gaze was drawn to a young couple at a nearby table.

"Look to your right," she said in a tone barely above a whisper. "Five bucks says it's their first date."

Jude leaned back in his chair and casually cast a sideways glance. A slow smile spread over his lips at the sight of the early-twenty-something young man sitting rigidly straight, Adam's apple bobbing, while the woman across from him with the too-bright eyes laughed nervously.

"Ah." Jude's eyes held sympathy. "The getting acquainted phase. Glad we're past that point."

"I disagree." Gabi lifted her glass of club soda. "There's still so much about each other we don't know."

"Well, I'm an open book." Jude grinned. "So, Miss Mysterious, tell me something I don't know about you."

I've had a heart transplant.

For a moment Gabi feared she'd spoken aloud. But when Jude reached across the table and took her hand, smiling encouragingly, she released her breath.

"C'mon, Gabi," he prompted. "One little-known fact."

She opened her mouth, fully prepared to tell him she only liked books with happy endings.

"I'm strong," she said instead. "I have this inner strength. I firmly believe I have it in me to handle whatever life throws my way."

"Confidence is such an appealing character trait." Jude caressed her palm with his thumb. "And so incredibly sexy."

Gabi's heart thumped. "You think everything is sexy."

His gaze caught hers and held. "Everything that concerns you, anyway."

Though she changed the subject and kept it light until their meals arrived, the air between them sizzled. Gabi's gaze kept returning to Jude. Each time their eyes met, the temperature in the room jumped thirty degrees. She was in the midst of one of those spikes of heat when the jarring sound of a tinny calypso beat broke the spell.

"Sorry." Gabi huffed out a breath. "Incoming text."

She reached into her purse, pulled out her phone and quickly read the message.

"Is everything okay?" Concern filled Jude's eyes.

"I told my father you were taking me out for dinner, so I'm surprised he—" Gabi paused. "On second thought, I'm not surprised. He knew very well he'd be interrupting—"

She handed the phone to Jude. "With a totally unimportant update."

Jude scanned the text, handed back the phone, smiled. "Sounds as if he's having a good evening. It was nice of Sawyer and Laurel to stop by to see him."

Gabi savored a bite of asparagus seasoned with basil and rosemary and tamped down her irritation. She would not let her father's meddling affect the evening. "I don't know if you realize it but the Mendozas and the Red Rock Fortunes have been close for generations."

"Really?"

Gabi continued to nibble on the asparagus. Nodded. "There have been three marriages between the families."

An amused smile hovered on the edges of Jude's lips. "Sounds like someone has done her research."

"Actually, my father was in an extremely talkative mood one morning—" Gabi stopped, realizing she'd once again brought her *father* into the conversation. Pretty soon, Jude would be suggesting they drive to Lubbock and visit him.

"Your dad always seems to have something to say."

Gabi grinned good-naturedly. "Here's what I know." She lifted a hand and raised one finger. "Roberto Mendoza is married to Frannie Fortune."

Jude's fork stopped just short of his mouth. He thought for a moment then nodded. "Okay."

Another finger popped up. "Roberto's cousin Isabel is married to J. R. Fortune."

Jude took a bite of baked potato, chewed, swallowed.

"Hmm" was all he said.

"Lastly." Gabi raised a third finger. "Wendy

Fortune is married to Marcos Mendoza. This adds up to three marriages between the two families."

"Well done." Jude lifted his glass of wine in a type of salute. "I believe you know more about the Fortune family than I do."

Something in his tone caught her interest. While he appeared to get on well with his cousin Sawyer, Jude rarely spoke of his connection with the Fortunes of Red Rock. In fact, she realized he rarely mentioned that branch of his family at all.

This was one area where Jude wasn't an open book. "I've never asked how you feel about being a Fortune."

Jude placed his wineglass on the table and shrugged. "It's simply a name. But family means a lot to my mom. That's why I went along with her request to take the Fortune name. Carrying it doesn't change a thing. I'm the same person I've always been—Deke Jones's son."

"Your father is a great guy." Gabi toyed with her fork. "It takes a special man to agree to let his children bear the Fortune name."

"I've said it before and I'll say it again, my dad would do anything for my mom." Jude's tone was matter-of-fact.

Gabi thought of her own parents. "My father was equally devoted to my mother."

Dear God, had she really brought up her *father* again?

"Was it hard for Orlando to leave Miami?"

"In some ways this was like coming home for him. Remember, he lived in Texas until he was ten. My brothers and I were sad to see him move, but we believed the change of pace and the chance to be more involved with flying would be good for him." Gabi's fingers tightened around her fork. "None of us could have predicted his move would result in a near-death experience."

She blinked away sudden tears.

Jude said nothing, only reached over and gave her hand a squeeze.

"The accident only reinforced that life is precious," she murmured, almost to herself. "We need to savor every moment."

That's what she'd do tonight, Gabi promised herself. She'd enjoy every second of the time she had left with Jude.

Music smooth as warm cream filled the air. Couples rose and headed to a dance floor where cascades of shiny red foil hearts hung from the ceiling.

Jude pushed back his chair and held out his hand. "May I have this dance?"

"Since you ask so politely..." Gabi rose. When they reached the shiny wooden dance floor, Jude took her into his arms in a natural, experienced movement.

She fit perfectly against him and discovered there was something incredibly romantic about being dressed up with a real band playing in the background and shiny red hearts hanging overhead.

By the time the set ended and they returned to the table, the dishes had been cleared and the waiter appeared for their dessert order.

Gabi politely declined dessert and the waiter's offer of a postdinner coffee. Jude ordered both.

Once they were alone again, she turned to Jude. "Did I mention I spoke with Steve earlier today?"

Jude's blue eyes cooled. "I don't believe you did."

Gabi took a sip of water. "He called when I was getting ready for tonight. He said The Garden was an excellent choice for dinner."

"Glad to have his approval." Jude gave a sardonic smile. "What did he want?"

"Apparently there's a big animal extravaganza at the Civic Center in Lubbock on Sunday. He asked if I'd be interested in manning the shelter's booth in the afternoon. There will be several adoptable dogs in the booth with me."

Jude toyed with the stem of his wineglass. "What did you tell him?"

"I said yes, *we'd* be interested." She offered Jude a slow smile. "Not inviting you was, I'm sure, a simple oversight on his part. After all, we are going steady...."

The lines between Jude's brows that had appeared at the mention of Steve's name eased. He grinned.

Before Jude could say anything, the waiter returned to set up a mini dessert station tableside. Gabi watched him expertly combine then cook brown sugar, cinnamon, butter and banana liqueur in a small pan over a medium flame. Bananas were added and once the waiter appeared satisfied they were properly tender, dark rum was added to the pan and ignited. The mixture was served over a scoop of ice cream.

"It looks delicious." Gabi smiled at the waiter when he placed the dessert in front of Jude.

Though she'd insisted she didn't want any dessert, Jude dipped a second spoon into the dish and handed it to her. "The first bite is yours."

Gabi didn't argue. She shut her eyes and let herself savor the perfect blending of flavors. When she opened her eyes, she found Jude staring.

She licked the last traces of sugar off her lips with the tip of her tongue. "It's superb. You're going to love it."

With his eyes firmly fixed on her, Jude took a bite. "It is good."

He dipped his spoon into the dish then held it out to her.

She stared longingly but shook her head.

"You're right. This isn't what I'm hungry for, either." He lowered the spoon, stared into her eyes. "I want to make love with you, Gabi."

Her heart began to pound as the desire for him that she'd kept under tight control rose inside her like a tidal wave. Gabi held out a hand and let him draw her to her feet.

For tonight, he would be hers.

Chapter 12

The short drive to Horseback Hollow seemed to take an eternity. In the truck, Gabi sizzled with pent-up need and intense desire for the man beside her.

To distract herself, she attempted to make conversation, asking about the lights twinkling in the distance.

"There's a lot of building going on around Vicker's Corners," Jude explained. "New condominiums and luxury homes, designed to lure those who want country quiet but also to be near their jobs in Lubbock."

While he spoke, he took her hand, caressing the palm with his thumb. When silence fell again and the simmering heat in the truck reached low boil, he brought her fingers to his lips and kissed her knuckles. The warm, moist touch of his mouth against her skin had sensation licking up her arm, down her breasts and on down to pool between her thighs.

"I wish we were there now." Gabi squirmed in her seat as her blood beat a primal rhythm.

He slanted a sideways glance. "Things might progress more quickly once we get to the ranch, if we do some preplanning."

The tone of his voice implied what he had in mind was something she might really like.

Gabi didn't need to feign interest. "What did you have in mind?"

"For starters, shedding some clothes." The boyish smile he shot her held a roguish edge. "I'd gladly participate but I have to drive."

He wore her favorite cologne and, in the close confines of the truck cab, she could smell something else; soap and that indefinable warm male scent that made her want to throw herself at him and agree to anything he asked. "What are you suggesting I take off?"

"Your dress. Or a piece of underwear," he said with an innocent expression. "Completely up to you."

"I prefer not to get arrested for indecent exposure," she said in a haughty tone that somehow managed to sound provocative.

"Appears the choice is clear."

Gabi liked teasing with him about such things, liked the shivering, sliding feeling that ran down her spine. She liked the way her blood hummed at the mere thought of removing her panties while he sat behind the wheel less than two feet from her. Of course she wasn't going to take off her underwear. Though the thought was intriguing....

"I had a friend during my freshman year in college who used to leave off her underwear when going on a date. She said it made her feel sexy." Gabi gave a throaty laugh. "I thought she was crazy."

"Did you try it?"

"I never did." That had been shortly before she'd caught the virus. Her boyfriend had vanished, and it had been a long time before Gabi thought of anything other than doctor visits and antirejection regimens.

"Perhaps it's time to be adventurous and give it a try." His eyes looked as dark as hers in the dim light, his words practically daring her to step off the safe shores of what she'd always known into a place where she could be over her head in seconds.

"What do you have to lose?" Jude asked, his voice smooth and persuasive.

Gabi's heart stuttered. She liked to think of

herself as the adventurous sort. Besides, if she did as he suggested, it wasn't as if he—or anyone else—could see there wasn't anything beneath her dress but bare skin.

Telling herself not to overthink, Gabi turned in her seat and wiggled out of the silky panties, giving Jude a flash of her upper thigh.

She dangled the black satin-and-lace thong between two fingers, waving them the way a bullfighter might toss a cape. "Voilà."

In an instant, Jude had snagged the tiny scrap of fabric from her hand, rolled down the window and her pretty underwear disappeared into the night.

"Hey." Her voice took on a clip of annoyance. "I liked those."

His smile was smug and unrepentant. "I'll buy you more."

The thought of Jude Fortune Jones walking into Victoria's Secret in cowboy boots and hat to buy lingerie had her irritation melting away. She chuckled. "I'm going to hold you to that promise."

"Darlin'," he said in a sexy drawl that wrapped itself around her spine and caused an inward shudder. "I wouldn't expect less."

For a moment they sat silently. Gabi made a great show of straightening her dress. She smiled at Jude. "I don't feel any different going commando."

The use of the phrase seemed to make him smile. He lifted a brow and shot her a look that clearly questioned her veracity.

Well, perhaps she did feel a teeny-weeny bit wicked. And, when he looked at her with that heat in his eyes, the knowledge that she was naked beneath the dress did cause some different and interesting sensations to course through her body. "Okay, a little different."

His smile widened.

By the time they reached his ranch, Gabi understood her college friend a whole lot better.

Of course Jude had only continued to fan the flames smoldering inside her. Every topic they discussed could have or did have something to do with sex.

He spoke of the fence they were replacing in the north pasture, which made her think of their trail ride. Then he mentioned his sisters had gone shopping in Lubbock, which brought to mind her missing panties. Then there was the new bull...

By the time Jude pulled the truck to a stop and got out, Gabi ached for him, wanted him with a desperate intensity she'd never experienced.

He obviously felt the same. They barely made it inside before his mouth was on hers, his hands groping her through the lacy fabric.

"Take this off," he said, tugging at the dress.

"Not here." She pushed his hands away, her breath coming in short puffs. "Not with your mom watching us from over there."

Startled, Jude jerked his head toward the fireplace then expelled a breath at the sight of the family portrait of his family smiling back at them.

"You're right," he agreed. "Not here."

Jude grabbed her hand and began to pull her toward the bedroom. Once they reached the hall, he jerked her back to him and began kissing her—urgent, fevered kisses that matched the wild beat in his blood.

Raw need urged him to take her now, against the wall, on the floor. But he resisted, telling himself she deserved better than a wild tumble.

They stumbled into the bedroom, bodies and mouths melded together. Still pressed together, he reached over and flipped on the light.

She switched it off.

"In the dark," she insisted against his mouth. "Just the first time."

At that moment, she could have asked him to do it standing on his head and Jude would have done his best to comply.

The shades were drawn, which, considering the proximity to the neighboring house, was totally unnecessary. The room was pitch-black other than a distant glow from the light in the living room.

Though her passion appeared as ferocious as his, the way she'd blushed in the truck when he first suggested shedding her panties told him she didn't have a lot of experience.

Through the haze of mounting desire, Jude found himself glad of the fact and determined she wouldn't regret trusting him with her body and with her heart. While she'd never said she cared, he knew she'd never let him get this close if she didn't.

He tightened his hold on his control and forced himself to speak softly in the same tone he used with a skittish colt. "Let me undress you. There's no reason to rush."

"I don't want slow." Heat vibrated in her voice. "You're lucky to have made it through the front door without me knocking you down and having my way with you."

Jude laughed, pulled her face up for a long, hard kiss. "You're something special, Gabi Mendoza."

"Yes, I am." She tugged at his suit jacket. "And you have way too many clothes on. Strip."

"It'd be easier if I could see," Jude muttered as he fumbled with his belt. Yet, the urgent need for her propelled his movements and his clothes quickly found their way to the floor.

"Easier isn't better." She moved to him. "Neither is slower."

When Jude wrapped his arms around her and felt only warm, fragrant skin, he realized she was already naked. *Almost* naked. By her position in his arms, she was obviously still wearing her heels.

If he hadn't already been hard, the mental image of her nude except for high heels would have sent him careening wildly in that direction.

"This is my favorite dance so far." Torturing him with her nearness, Gabi hummed one of the songs they'd dipped and swayed to at The Garden, while her body rubbed sensuously against his in all the best places.

Jude slid his hand into her tangled mass of curls. "I want you."

"I hope so," she murmured, "or I lost a perfectly good pair of panties for no reason."

Gabi felt some of her nervousness fade at his quick laugh. The touch of his knuckles against her cheek was wildly erotic.

"Jude." She spoke his name, then paused, not sure what she wanted to say.

Love me as much as I love you?

Please don't love me because I can't bear the thought of hurting you?

"I want you," he repeated, his voice a husky

caress. Not quite steady fingers touched the curve
of her cheek, trailed along the line of her jaw.

"I want you more." It was the truth. Her need
for him was a stark carnal hunger she hadn't
known she was capable of feeling. She'd never
wanted anything or anyone as much as she
wanted Jude Fortune Jones.

He ran his palms up along her sides, skimming the curve of her breasts. Gabi arched back
while his long fingers lifted and supported her
yielding flesh as his thumbs brushed across the
tight points of her nipples.

His stroking fingers sent shock waves of feeling through her body. The melody she'd been
humming died away on a soft little whimper as
her knees went weak.

Scooping her up in his arms he carried her to
the bed then dropped down beside her.

"If you were tired, all you had to do was say
so." Her voice sounded breathless even to her
ears.

He chuckled. "I've learned that when knees
go weak, it's best to be horizontal."

Before she had a chance to respond, he folded
her more fully into his arms, anchoring her
against his chest as his mouth covered hers in a
deep, compelling kiss.

Then his palms were once again on the move,
skimming the curve of her breasts before he al-

lowed the tips of his fingers the barest of contact with her flesh.

Her nipples stiffened, straining toward the remembered delight of his touch even as the warmth in her lower belly turned fiery hot and became a pulsating need.

She longed to run her hands over his body, to feel the coiled strength of skin and muscle sliding under her fingers. She wanted him to touch her in the same way, wanted to feel the weight of his body on hers. Wanted to feel him inside her.

Gabi planted an urgent kiss at the base of his neck, his skin salty beneath her lips.

His hand flattened against her lower back, drawing her up against the length of his body.

"You are beautiful," he whispered into her ear right before he took the lobe between his teeth and nibbled.

Shivers rippled across her skin.

"You're soft," he continued as he kissed below her ear, then down her throat. One of his hands lightly stroked her belly.

His hand moved up, pausing when it encountered the raised ridge of her scar. She tensed, but then his mouth replaced his hand and he was kissing his way up, touching his tongue to the tip of her left breast.

It was dark and all she could see was the outline of his head. But the combination of seeing and feeling was the most erotic experience of her life. Gabi cried out in delight.

He circled her nipple then drew it fully into his mouth. The gentle sucking had her arching against him. At the same time, his hand dipped low, slipping through her curls and between her legs.

She parted for him, catching her breath as he rubbed against her slick center, then slipped one, then two fingers inside her. When he shifted slightly and found that single spot of pleasure, she nearly rose off the bed.

This was like before, when they'd been on the trail ride, but more intense. She couldn't bear herself enough to him. She wanted to be more naked, more exposed, more intimate.

"Don't stop," she breathed, her blood like a fever in her veins.

Thankfully, he didn't. He continued to touch her, stroking her, teasing, circling as he worshipped her breasts. The combination made her mind go blank, her breathing come in hard pants. "I want you inside me."

She didn't have to ask twice.

Gabi heard the rustle of a condom packet being torn open, or at least that's what she assumed it was, then he was inside her.

He was large and stretched her in the best

way possible. She felt filled, yet the need for more grew.

He wrapped his arms around her, drawing her close so they pressed together everywhere. She clung to him, urging him deeper.

"More," she breathed as he withdrew only to fill her again.

The rhythmic thrusting made her pulse against him. She couldn't get enough. She strained toward him, needing, wanting. She dropped her hands to his hips to pull him closer.

She hadn't known that this much pleasure existed in the world. That she could feel so good, so right, so everything.

Her pulse throbbed hard and thick. Gabi tried to catch her breath then gave up air completely as her release claimed her.

The climax rippled through her and still he touched her, gentling the contact until the last breath had been wrung from her body. At the very end, when she was sure there couldn't be anything else, he shuddered in her embrace and called out her name.

If Gabi hadn't known, hadn't had all the tests reassuring her that her heart was good and strong, the rapid pounding in her chest would have worried her. Yet, despite the *thump, thump,*

thump, languid warmth filled her limbs as she lay curled in Jude's arms.

"That was," she said as she kissed his neck, "quite spectacular."

"I aim to please."

In the darkness, she felt his smile against her cheek.

"Do you want to tell me about it?" His voice was as warm and soothing as his arms.

Still, Gabi stiffened. "About?"

"The scar." He shifted, gathered her closer, kissed her temple. "I've seen scars before, you know. You don't grow up with four brothers and not get them. We used to call them badges of honor."

She could hear the hint of laughter in his voice.

"Why badges of honor?"

"Because they signified that you'd forged ahead, given whatever you were tackling your all, even if what you were tackling was one of your brothers." This time he did release a chuckle as his hand gently stroked her back.

Badge of honor. She might have to think of her scar in those terms. God knows, when faced with the situation, she'd forged ahead, given it her all, and came out whole on the other side.

Between them the silence stretched and extended, but Gabi didn't feel any pressure. She sensed that Jude would give her all the time she needed. He was kind. A good man.

"I had to have heart surgery." Gabi closed her eyes, breathed deep. "When I was nineteen. It, ah, fixed the problem, but left me with quite a scar."

The gentle glide of his palm up and down her spine paused for a fraction of a second then continued. "You're okay now?"

"Like new." Gabi told herself it wasn't a lie. In a way, it was true.

He exhaled a breath, pulling her tight against him for a moment. "Good."

Gabi thought she could be content to lie here with his arms around her until, say, the next millennium.

"Can I see your scar?" he asked.

She knew he felt her tense; she wasn't a good enough actress to keep her emotions that hidden. It irritated her that she could feel so vulnerable just because of the incident at the pool party.

"Not your scar," he corrected. "Your badge of honor. If you show me yours, I'll show you mine."

"You have a scar?"

"Darlin', every Jones boy has scars." He kissed her hair. "I've got one from an emergency appendectomy when I was nine that will blow yours out of the water."

"We'll just have to see about that."

"Okay, then." Still, Jude made no move to get up. "Tell me why I mentioned turning on the lights, when I'm so nice and comfortable right where I am."

"It's your curious nature." Gabi trailed a fingertip up his arm. "Trust me, that'll kick you in the balls every time."

His eyes widened in mock surprise. He leaned back, holding her at arm's length. "Miss Mendoza, does your father know you use such language?"

Gabi liked this playful side of Jude. But then she liked his serious side, his sexy side… She forced her thoughts back to the question.

"Who do you think I first heard that from?" She grinned. "And don't even try to tell me Stacey and Delaney haven't picked up a few of those kernels of wisdom from your dad and brothers."

"Guilty." Jude gave her a quick pat on the bottom as he rose and crossed the room to the light switch.

She expected the room to be immediately flooded with stark white light. The kind she remembered from the O.R. suites. Instead, Jude must have had a dimmer switch because the room definitely lightened, but no more than 30 or 40 percent.

Gabi decided she must still be basking in the

afterglow of lovemaking because the light reminded her of golden moonlight.

Jude returned to bed, crawling in beside her, pulling her close once again. His blond hair looked as if someone had raked their fingers through it. Gabi smiled, realizing that someone was her.

His cheeks were dark with a light scrabble of whiskers, but those blue eyes were clear and oh-so-blue when they latched on to hers. "Who goes first?"

"You," she said. "So you can revel in being the best for a few seconds until my scar—er, badge of honor—blows yours out of the water."

"Ah, more talk of scars." His eyes danced. "Stirs me up."

"Let's see it."

Jude glanced down. "It's a bit wilted at the moment but—"

"Not that," she said, swallowing a laugh. "Your appendectomy scar."

He exhaled an exaggerated sigh. "If that's what really interests you—"

"For the moment," she said. "But hold the other thought. We can revisit that in a moment."

He rolled to his back, the sheet riding low on his hips. There, slashing a raised pink swath down his right side was his badge of honor. "Pretty impressive."

Gabi leaned forward for a closer look, trailed a finger down the ridge of it. Then impulsively leaned close and pressed her lips over it. As she lifted her head, she felt tears sting her eyes. "You could have died. If they had to do emergency surgery it meant the appendix was ready to burst."

"It was," he agreed, wiping back the tears with the pads of his thumbs, his voice gentle. "But it didn't. The way I see it, we can't worry about what might have happened or what could happen. We have to take life one day at a time."

Feeling foolish, Gabi blinked back the tears.

"Hey." He cupped her face with his hand, his eyes boring into hers. "It means a lot to me that you care."

When she smiled, he put a serious expression on his face. "I've showed you mine. Now you show me yours."

Gabi loosened the death hold she had on the sheet she'd pulled to her neck the second the lights came on. She took a deep breath before ever-so-slowly lowering the sheet.

Jude's expression remained impassive as he took in the scar that started just a few inches below her throat and shot down between her breasts to a spot midabdomen. He cocked his head.

"Well, it is longer than mine. I'll give you

that," he said finally. "But it's also thinner and not as ropy."

He lifted his gaze. "I think we have a draw."

"It doesn't disgust you?"

Surprise flickered across his face. "Disgust? Why would it disgust me?"

Gabi vividly recalled the pool party held at a coworker's home. When she'd taken off her cover-up, she'd been shocked at the horrified looks by several new staff members. Until that moment, she'd never thought of her scar as ugly. But she'd seen several eyes widen and had even heard someone gasp. When the guy she was with grimaced and told her it was a total turnoff, she'd wanted to sink into the ground. Instead she'd told him his attitude was a total turnoff and walked away.

"It's ugly," she said finally.

He lifted his hands, looking truly puzzled. "It's simply a scar. Actually, a mighty good-looking one."

The tight grip around her chest began to ease. Jude might be somewhat adept at hiding his emotions, but she'd have known if he'd been horrified by what he was viewing.

Simply a scar.

Relief flooded her. "Now that our contest is over, I suggest we return to more important matters."

His lazy smile did strange things to her insides. "What did you have in mind?"

Gabi slipped her hand beneath the sheet, closed around him, found him in…full bloom. "I think we're on the same wavelength."

His arms encircled her. "Darlin', we are and have been…from the second we met."

Chapter 13

Sunday proved to be warm and sunny. Gabi stared into her closet pondering what to wear that afternoon to the Animal Extravaganza at the Lubbock Civic Center. Knowing she'd be around dogs all afternoon, she didn't want to get too dressed up. Yet, with Jude coming with her, she wanted to look nice.

No longer needing to hide her scar from him, Gabi chose a sage-colored top with a slightly scooped neck. The lightness of the fabric hinted at spring, but the three-quarter-length sleeves said the wearer understood the season hadn't yet arrived.

Gabi paired the top with a pair of jeans that made her waist look thin, her hips curved and her backside well toned—the perfect trifecta. Her only concession to style—and to the hope of spring—was a pair of strappy sandals with a touch of bling.

Pulling her hair back into a low ponytail, she studied her reflection then added a little lipstick.

Her mouth curved upward as she topped the color with some gloss. She didn't know why she bothered. Jude would have it all kissed off by the time they arrived at the Civic Center.

Man, did he like to kiss. And being the honest sort, Gabi had to admit she liked kissing him, too. They'd certainly done plenty of it in the past forty-eight hours.

When she wasn't with her father, she'd been with Jude. Last night, when the handsome cowboy who she'd begun to secretly think of as hers asked her to stay over, she'd told him yes.

Once her father was discharged and able to manage on his own, she'd be leaving Horseback Hollow. In the meantime, Gabi would cram in as much time with Jude as possible.

Take this morning. She'd sat with him in his family pew and had been seriously tempted when he'd invited her back to his parents' house for Sunday brunch.

In the end she'd begged off, telling him she had to call her brothers and update them on Orlando's progress. Though her father spoke—and texted—regularly with each of his sons, he didn't always give them a clear picture of his progress. The boys—er, men—depended on their little sister for unbiased, factual information.

After giving the same basic report and answering the same questions four different times, Gabi felt as if her day was finally ready to begin. She glanced at the clock on the wall and frowned. Jude was late.

Considering they still had to swing by the animal shelter and pick up the three dogs they'd be taking with them to the Civic Center then drive an hour to Lubbock, every minute counted if they wanted to be there when the Animal Extravaganza opened.

She pulled out her phone to text Jude but stopped when she heard his truck pull into the driveway. Through the front window she saw him get out, looking mouthwateringly handsome in jeans and a white polo, and quivered like a sixteen-year-old about to embark on a first date.

He took her hands and stepped back. "You look amazing."

Before she could respond, he leaned over and brought his lips to hers in a long, lingering kiss.

Stepping back, Jude stroked one hand up her arm as if he couldn't keep from touching her. "I've missed you."

"We just saw each other a couple hours ago,"

she said, even as she found herself linking her fingers with his.

"Feels like forever," he said, then kissed her again.

Warmth spread through Gabi's body, and she realized it was the same for her. How had he become so important in such a short time? All she thought about was him. Only when he was with her did her world feel in sync.

Better get used to it being out of sync, she scolded herself then grabbed a jacket. "We should get moving. We still have to stop by the shelter and—"

"All done." The eyes Jude fixed on her were curious and she worried they saw too much. "Dogs are in the truck."

"What? How?" Gabi asked then waved away the questions. "It doesn't matter."

Once outside, she hurried to the pickup. Jude had stowed the three carriers in the backseat of the truck's extended cab. Two held small dogs, while the other was in the medium to large size range. Or perhaps he just looked large, she thought, in comparison to the others.

"Is that a Shih Tzu?" She gestured to a black-and-white puffball calmly licking a paw.

"Yes." Jude paused, as if searching his memory. "That's Ernie. Nine-year-old male. The elderly woman who owned him died recently.

Apparently none of the family could take him. He's got papers and everything."

Gabi let her gaze linger on the small dog with big brown eyes, who'd recently lost the person he loved most in the world. Soon, very soon, she'd be in the position of being separated from the one she loved. Although Jude would still be alive, he wouldn't be with her.

"I'll find you a good home, Ernie," she said with an intensity that made Jude look up from the carrier he was straightening. "I promise."

The dog's fluffy tail thumped against the bottom of the crate, his big eyes full of trust.

Gabi took a steadying breath and shifted her gaze to the large carrier, the one holding the bigger dog. His sleek black fur was laced with silver and his golden eyes shone sharp and assessing. The animal's penetrating gaze never wavered from her face. "Who is this?"

"Shug."

Tilting her head, Gabi frowned. "That's his name?"

"Yep." Jude lifted a shoulder. "It was on his collar. He was a stray. He's a blue heeler, also known as an Australian cattle dog."

"I'd think with all your cattle, you could use one of these around your place."

"We already have a couple of border collies." Jude's blue eyes were warm and reassuring as he reached over and squeezed her hand. "Don't worry. We won't have any trouble finding this fella a good home."

The blue heeler must have finished his assessment of Gabi because his tail began to move slowly side to side, although his yellow eyes remained watchful.

"Jude is right," she told the animal. "We'll find you a home on a ranch. You can run and do whatever it is that cattle dogs do."

A low whine drew Gabi's attention to the last crate. It held a scruffy dog with longish hair and an even longer body. He stood, pawing at the metal door to the carrier as if saying, *Let me out, let me out*.

Gabi put her hand to the wire door and the plume of a tail shifted into high gear even as the animal's tongue snaked out in welcome.

"This one is a real cutie." Gabi shifted her gaze back to Jude. "What's his story?"

"Apparently some girl got him from her boyfriend as a gift. The girl moved out of state and the mother didn't want him." Jude smiled as the dog's whole body began to vibrate. "Best guess is he's a mix between a wire-haired dachshund and a Yorkshire terrier. The volunteer at the shelter called him a dorkie."

Gabi wrinkled her nose. "Dorkie?"

"Dachshund, Yorkie…dorkie." Jude chuckled. "His name is Chico, which doesn't fit, either."

"You're right. It sounds more like a Chihuahua or a Mexican hairless."

At the sound of his name, the dog began to whine again, pressing his scruffy face against the wire.

Jude glanced at his watch. "We best get on the road. Parking can be an issue around the Civic Center."

When Gabi stepped back, Chico crouched down and began to whimper, his dark eyes pleading.

Impulsively, Gabi opened the cage door. The dog sprang into her arms, slathering her face with doggy kisses. Keeping a firm hold on his wiggling body, Gabi ignored Jude's amused chuckle and took Chico with her to the front.

After securing the other doors, Jude climbed in behind the wheel. "Do you plan to hold him all the way to Lubbock?"

Chico, now relaxed, lay on his back, eyes closed as she stroked his belly.

"Maybe." Gabi smiled down at the dog. "I guess that will depend on how he tolerates the ride."

"He's liking where he's at right now," Jude observed.

Gabi shot him a wink. "If you're a good boy, I may rub *your* belly tonight."

Jude backed the truck out of the driveway and grinned. "This day just keeps getting better."

Before their shift was half-over at the Civic Center, Jude and Gabi had a rancher interested in Shug and an older couple in Ernie. Both had filled out the paperwork and set up times on Monday to stop by the shelter.

Jude fully believed they could have found a home for Chico, too, if Gabi hadn't been so determined to keep him out of sight. After they'd secured homes for Shug and Ernie, he told Gabi they should put Chico out front in the booth, engage people in conversation, let the lovable nature of the "dorkie" shine through.

Shortly after he made his suggestion, Gabi decided to take Chico for a walk. Jude noticed she took off the dog's red Adopt Me vest before leaving the booth.

She wants him, he thought.

Jude could already picture the little terrier running across the pastures, chasing the cats that'd soon show him who was boss. Though they'd mostly had big dogs growing up, Jude figured he wouldn't mind a small one. Not if that made Gabi happy.

While she strolled the exhibition hall aisles, picking up small bags of food from pet food distributors and other samples, Jude kept busy.

People stopped and added their email addresses to the shelter's electronic newsletter list. He talked up the fact they were a no-kill shelter and passed out flyers containing pictures and blurbs on the animals back at the shelter eager for a "forever home."

A forever home. That's what Jude wanted with Gabi. He thought about all those times he'd been convinced he was in love and realized whatever he'd felt for those women had been but a pale imitation of what he felt for her.

He could be himself with Gabi. There wasn't anything they couldn't talk about, anything they couldn't share, anything they couldn't work out. The incident with the scars was a perfect example of the level of trust that existed between them.

His jaw tightened as he remembered the flash of fear in her eyes when she slowly lowered the sheet. Someone in the past had made some nasty comment about the scar, he was sure of it. That incident had made her so self-conscious she hadn't wanted anyone to see it.

Yet, for the first time since they'd met, today she'd worn a shirt that didn't wrap around her neck. He'd wanted to cheer. He briefly considered making some teasing comment about how good it was to see the scar come out of the closet. After a second's hesitation, he'd kept his mouth shut. The last thing he wanted was for her to think the scar was the first thing anyone noticed.

No one had said anything to her today, he thought with a smile of satisfaction. He was sure most of them didn't even notice it. They were too focused on her irresistible smile and her enthusiasm for the animals.

Besides, he meant what he'd said the other night. It was a badge of honor. She'd fought heart disease and won.

"How's it going?"

Jude jerked his head up and saw Steve at the entrance to the booth. Instead of the jeans he and Gabi had worn, the bank executive wore a brown suit and looked ready to conduct a presentation to his board of directors. "It's going good. I didn't expect you so soon."

Steve ignored the comment and glanced around. "Where's Gabi?"

"She's checking out the exhibition area." As far as Jude was concerned, now that Steve was here, she could take her sweet time returning to the booth. "Until ten minutes ago we were swamped. Traffic is finally beginning to slow down."

"Did you generate any interest in the animals you brought?" Steve gestured with his head toward the two crates where Ernie and Shug slept.

"We found homes for both of them." Jude glanced to a manila folder on the counter. "Both prospective owners filled out the paperwork and plan to stop by the shelter tomorrow to complete the adoption process."

"I thought you were going to bring three." Steve leaned casually against the table.

"We've decided to adopt the dachshund-Yorkie mix," Jude said without thinking, then watched Steve's brows rise.

"We?"

"Gabi," Jude clarified in a matter-of-fact tone. "She wants him. But if her dad gives her grief, I have plenty of room at the ranch for the little guy."

"Appears things between you and the lovely Ms. Mendoza are heating up," Steve said with a slow, lazy smile. "My aunt Alma lives down the street from Gabi's father. She mentioned Gabi has recently started sleeping elsewhere."

Damn.

He should have thought things through, Jude thought, furious with himself. Horseback Hollow was a small town where neighbors watched out for each other. Of course they'd be keeping an eye on Orlando's house. Especially considering the man was in Lubbock and his daughter was in an unfamiliar town all alone.

Jude wondered how long it would take for someone to mention the overnight sleepovers to Gabi's dad.

"O worries about his daughter," Jude said, his gaze pointed. "I'd hate for him to get wind of anything that might upset him."

Steve shrugged. "Hey, there are no secrets in a small town."

"Hi, Steve." Gabi strolled up with Chico on a leash at her side. "We didn't expect you until five."

"It's a beautiful day." Steve shot Gabi a speculative glance. "I thought you and Jude might want to enjoy what's left of it."

"That's kind of you."

"Who's this little guy?" Steve crouched down, extended a hand to the scruffy dog, which the animal carefully sniffed.

"His name is Chico." Gabi began to stammer. "I forgot his Adopt Me sweater and came back for it."

"Wouldn't putting it on be false advertising?" Steve pulled to his feet.

"I don't know what you mean."

"Jude told me you're planning to adopt him." Gabi's gaze darted to Jude.

"I said you wanted him," Jude explained. "If your father doesn't like the idea of a dog in his home, I'll take him."

"You'd do that?"

Jude wished Steve wasn't there, watching so intently and obviously listening to every word. If they were alone, he'd tell Gabi he'd do anything to make her happy. He settled for a simple, "Of course."

For a second, Jude thought Gabi was going to fling herself into his arms.

"Hear that, Chico?" Gabi scooped up the dog and hugged him instead. "You're my boy now."

"Take him home with you," Steve urged, waving a magnanimous hand. "You can complete all the paperwork later."

"It's official," Gabi told the dog, who immediately began slathering her with kisses. "I'm your new mama."

Watching her gentleness with the animal, Jude felt his heart stir. Gabi would make a good mother. Their children would never lack for love.

"I need to swing by the shelter on my way back." Steve gestured to the crates where Shug and Ernie slept. "I can take these other two with me and drop them off. Have they been out to the pet relief area recently?"

"Less than a half hour ago," Jude told him. The grassy knoll out back of the exhibition hall had everything a dog could want—grass, trees, bushes and even a fake fire hydrant.

"Good. One more thing." Steve's phone beeped. Though he pulled it from his pocket, his eyes never left Gabi. "Our branch manager in Vicker's Corners told me today she's accepted a position in Dallas. I'd love to get someone with your credentials for that spot. If you decide to apply, let me know. I'll fast-track the application."

Gabi opened her mouth, then closed it and just smiled.

Gabi kept Chico on her lap during the drive back to Horseback Hollow. Apparently all the excitement of the day had tired him out. The dog slept, cuddled close to her.

Which is where he'd like to be, thought Jude. He liked the feel of Gabi's body against his, liked having her beside him when he woke in the morning. But for now, the overnight stays would have to end.

The last thing he wanted was for Gabi to be hurt by gossip. If word got back to Orlando that Gabi had been sleeping elsewhere while he was in rehab, there would be hell to pay.

Not that Jude could blame Orlando. If he had a daughter, he'd be protective, too. A sudden image of baby Piper flashed. Would Gabi and his child look like his niece? Or would their son or daughter inherit Gabi's beautiful brown eyes and thick dark hair?

"I'm not sure what my father is going to think when he hears I've brought a dog into his home."

Jude pulled his thoughts back to the present and slanted a sideways glance. Her hand continued to gently stroke the animal's wiry fur, and when the dog snorted in sleep, Gabi smiled.

"I'm sure he won't mind," Jude assured her. "After all, it's only temporary."

Temporary, because if Jude had his way, Gabi would soon be his wife. Once they were married, she and Chico would move into the ranch house.

"You're right." Her smile vanished. "Once my father comes home, I'll be back in Miami."

No, Jude thought, with a hint of panic. There was no reason for her to return to Miami when everything she needed was right here, including him.

"You've enjoyed your time in Horseback Hollow," he reminded her.

"I really have. I'd never been this far west before." She settled back against the leather seat. "I wasn't sure what to expect. I'd kept an open mind, but this—" she lifted a hand and swept the air "—was far different than what I imagined."

He waited for her to continue.

"The people are so friendly. They look you in the eye and smile when they pass you on the street." Gabi's voice grew more animated as she continued. "Though everyone dresses nicely, there isn't the emphasis on appearance and youth that I saw in Miami. At the bank where I work, women who weren't even forty were visiting cosmetic surgeons, worried about looking 'old.'"

"Unbelievable" was all he said.

"I know. It's insane." For a second she simply stared out the window. "While I love the ocean and the palms, I love the vastness of the terrain here. It will be hard to leave."

Just hearing her utter the words in such a matter-of-fact tone struck terror in Jude's heart. But he kept his voice calm. "Your father will miss you."

She sighed. "I know."

"My parents always encouraged us to find our own way." Jude slanted a sideways glance. "But they also showed us that at the end of the day it's not how much money you have or how big of a home you can afford to build—family is what matters."

"Do you think that's why your mother asked you to take on the Fortune name?" Gabi asked. "To show them that she values her connection with them? And, speaking of the Fortunes, has the NTSB determined yet if sabotage was involved in the crash?"

"To answer your first question, I believe the reason she wanted her children to incorporate the Fortune name was to show her acceptance of that connection. In terms of the second, the ruling on the crash is expected any day. But it's a government agency, so who really knows." Jude kept his impatience under wraps, wondering how the conversation had shifted from the importance of family and Horseback Hollow to the Fortunes.

Regardless, he was determined to get it back on track and make Gabi realize what was really important in life and all she'd be leaving behind.

Jude pulled into the driveway of her dad's home and cut the engine. Across the street, he caught sight of Alma standing in her yard pretending to inspect the branches of a bush that hadn't yet budded out. "Having you here matters to your father. Having you care enough to drop whatever else you were doing and come and be with him when he needed you, matters."

"I had to come." A look Jude couldn't quite decipher crossed her face. "He was there for me through my surgery and recovery. He's always been there for me. I wanted to be here for him."

Finally, Jude thought, the discussion was firmly back on track. Now all he had to do was get Gabi to realize that the connection with him also mattered. And, more importantly, to realize that he was someone she simply couldn't live without.

Chapter 14

The next week passed quickly with Orlando gaining strength and Gabi drawing closer to her favorite cowboy. Jude told her about neighbor Alma Peatry's eagle eyes. That put an end to the sleepovers. Though Gabi no longer spent the night, she and Jude found late afternoon with sunlight streaming through partially drawn shades was a perfect time to make love.

The increasing closeness they shared wasn't only in the bedroom. Every evening they took Chico for a walk, holding hands as they strolled down the sidewalk. One night they went to a renovated movie theater in Lubbock and sat in the back row. Gabi discovered the fun of eating popcorn and kissing a guy you were crazy about in a darkened theater.

During these long walks and times together, Jude told her about his childhood—amusing little anecdotes about his parents and brothers and sisters. Stories that helped her understand how he'd grown into the fine man he was today.

She did her own sharing, regaling him with stories about how during her father's deployments, her mother had kept the family's spirits up by playing practical jokes on her children. Though Gabi had gotten good at spotting the pranks and preempting them, her brothers had continued to be snookered each and every time.

She and Jude talked about how hard it had been to leave family and go off to college. As they spoke of those years away from home, Gabi found herself tempted to tell Jude about her transplant.

The fact that he was so honest with her only compounded her guilt over withholding the information from him.

In the end, it was fear that kept her lips sealed. Fear if she told him about her new heart, he wouldn't walk away. He'd stick.

The love she felt for him refused to let him make such a sacrifice. She wanted him happy. He'd get over her, she told herself, find someone to marry—

The mere thought of another woman with him was a dagger to her heart.

"Maybe I *could* stay," she told Chico, as she sat on the porch brushing his wiry hair.

She'd risen early, too restless to sleep, and decided to give the dorkie a bath and a good brushing before heading to Lubbock.

The dog looked up from his position on the step. She swore she saw the question in his eyes.

"Wherever I am, you'll be with me," she assured him. Gabi wasn't sure what her landlord would say. But her lease was up, so if she needed to move, this would be the time to do it. "But, darn it, Chico, I like it here. I think you feel the same."

The dog appeared to nod, although it may have been simply the pull of the brush against the top of his head.

"Jude is wonderful." Just saying his name made her heart stutter. "I've never known anyone like him. I'll never love anyone else."

A lump clogged her throat and tears filled her eyes. "I don't know how I can do without him, Chico."

At the sound of his name, the dog licked her hand, thumped his tail.

"You love him, too, don't you?"

A tear dribbled down her cheek. She hurriedly swiped it away. Alma continued to be a one-woman neighborhood watch. Gabi had no doubt she could spot reddened eyes from fifty yards.

"The thing is—" though there was no one but Chico around to hear, Gabi dropped her voice to a whisper "—I know he loves me, too."

While Jude may not have said the words, she saw the emotion each time she gazed into those oh-so-blue eyes.

"I was a fool," she told the dog, "to think I could have a simple fling with him."

She continued to brush the wiry coat while her mind replayed that first meeting with Jude. From the first instant, he'd charmed her. But it was the man beneath that charming exterior who'd captured her heart.

"The core problem remains." She expelled a heavy sigh. "I can't give him children. I can't guarantee I'll be around in another ten years."

Gabi knew the stats. Knew that less than 40 percent of heart transplant patients were alive twenty years posttransplant. Still, she'd been young and healthy when she'd gotten her heart and had already made it this far with no rejection. But then she thought of her friends and knew that was no guarantee.

Gabi could already envision what would happen if she attempted to sit down and explain why she couldn't be with him. He'd call her a worrywart. And, because he was the optimistic sort, he'd try to convince her she was overreacting, making a major decision about their future because of fear over something that might never occur.

He'd look up the statistics and quote them to illustrate he was correct in his optimism. Gabi knew those stats as well as she knew her own name.

The numbers could be considered encouraging. It was also true some transplant patients fared better than others. Several points in her favor were she'd made it seven years without a setback and took excellent care of her body.

But statistics didn't tell the whole story. Gabi thought of Kate and Mary, a couple of women she'd met online after her surgery. They'd had heart transplants around the same time as her and had appeared to do everything right. But Kate's heart had showed signs of rejection on a recent cardiac biopsy, and Mary had passed away shortly before Gabi arrived in Horseback Hollow.

"I saw the pain my father went through when he lost my mother." At the words, Chico merely thumped his tail and gave her another lick. "How can I knowingly put Jude in a position of having to face something like that?"

She glanced around the neighborhood. At the trees with tiny buds that would soon become leaves, at the bold green tips of flowers she couldn't even identify peeking their way through the rich soil, and desperately wished things could be different.

Perhaps she could simply stay in Horseback Hollow. She loved it here. It already felt like home to her.

She and Jude could continue to date. They didn't have to get serious....

The second the thought entered her mind, she rejected it. Though she'd like to believe keeping the relationship casual was possible, things were already serious.

Perhaps, she thought, grasping at straws, having kids wasn't a big deal to him. If she kept herself in good physical shape, she could keep the odds in her favor. Perhaps…

Her phone dinged. Gabi glanced at the fourth text she'd received from her father just that morning.

"Apparently the doctor is coming at two to discuss discharge plans," she told the dog. "I have to be there."

After texting her father she'd join him for lunch and stay until the doctor arrived, Gabi laid down the brush and picked up the small dog, hugging him until he squirmed. Though she'd learned long ago that wishing for something didn't make it so, those days preceding her transplant had also shown her the importance of hope.

This afternoon, she'd focus on her father. Then she'd decide what to do about Jude.

The tight set to her father's mouth when she walked into the dining area a little over an hour later told her today hadn't been any better for him than yesterday. Ever since the doctor had started talking discharge plans, his therapy had kicked into high gear.

When she'd visited yesterday, her father had been in a funk. He told her the therapists and nurses had no idea how hard he was working and certainly had little sympathy for his pain.

Though Gabi understood these past few days had been trying, by the time she'd headed back to Horseback Hollow last night, she had a pounding headache and her sympathies were firmly with the staff.

"Your food is probably cold by now," Orlando said in lieu of a greeting, pointing to a plate covered by a silver dome. "It's been sitting there for almost a half hour."

The nurse in the hall who Gabi had passed on her way to the dining room had told her she'd just brought in the guest tray, so it should be good and hot.

"I'm sorry I wasn't here sooner." Gabi brushed a quick kiss on her father's cheek then settled into the chair opposite him. "I gave Chico a bath and was brushing him when you called. I lost track of the time."

"I don't understand why you got a dog." Her father forked off a bite of meat loaf, scowled. "You know your landlord won't let you keep him."

"My lease is up." Gabi held on to her rising temper with both hands. She removed the silver topper from her food and separated the paper napkin from the utensils. "If I have to, I'll find a new place to live."

"You're going back, then."

Gabi looked at him in surprise. Ever since she'd arrived in Horseback Hollow, her father had been telling her she needed to get back to Florida. To her job. To her life there. Not going back had never been on the table.

Now he acted as if her staying was a possibility she'd been considering all along.

"My job is there." She forced a little laugh. "If I want to eat, I have to work."

"I heard Steve Watkins has an opening for a bank manager." For the first time since she'd walked into the dining room, the lines around his mouth relaxed. "It'd be nice to have you close. If you want to stay, that is. You know me. I don't interfere in my children's lives."

Since when? Gabi wanted to ask, but pressed her lips together until the impulse passed. "How did you hear about the bank job in Vicker's Corners?"

"I've got my sources." Orlando stabbed a green bean. "By the way, your boyfriend stopped by earlier."

Gabi's fingers froze on the napkin she'd been placing on her lap. "Jude?"

Her father's brow lifted. "You have more than one boyfriend?"

"No. But I thought Jude was busy moving cattle today." Gabi flushed. "And to clarify, Jude Fortune Jones and I are just friends."

"Look at these lines." Orlando pointed with his fork to his handsome, weathered face. "I wasn't born yesterday."

Her father's voice suddenly sounded almost jovial. The scowl he'd greeted her with only moments earlier had vanished.

Gabi took a bite of meat loaf, put it in her mouth and chewed for a moment. Orlando's change in mood appeared tied to the possibility of her remaining in Horseback Hollow permanently. Had it been Jude who'd planted that seed?

"Did Jude make a special trip to Lubbock to see you?" Though she tried to keep her tone nonchalant, the question sounded more like she was interrogating her father rather than asking a simple question about an unimportant topic.

"He may have mentioned something about

picking up supplies." Orlando took another bite of green beans, ignoring the pile of carrots on his plate.

Gabi sensed he was waiting for her to pepper him with questions. Instead she brought a couple of steamed baby carrots to her mouth then followed it with a sip of skim milk.

"He came up during my therapy," Orlando offered when she remained silent.

Gabi expelled the breath she didn't realize she'd been holding. Between her father's therapy and Jude's errands, it appeared there had been little time for the two men to do much more than exchange brief pleasantries.

Besides, even if they'd had more time, it wasn't as if Jude would have mentioned they were sleeping together. "Too bad he came when you were busy."

"He stayed and watched." Orlando's lips curved in a slight smile. "After observing the session, Jude agrees my therapist is a sadist."

It took a moment for the words to register. Gabi dropped her fork. "He did not say that."

Orlando shrugged. "He thought it. Know what else?"

Gabi was afraid to ask, but the way the conversation was going, she had the feeling her father would tell her anyway. She lifted her glass of milk. "What else?"

"The boy is in love with you, Gabriella."

The milk Gabi had been swallowing took a detour. She coughed, gasped, fought for breath. After a few seconds, she regained her composure. "Let me get this straight. He told you he loved me?"

"I have eyes," her father responded. "It'd be obvious to a blind man."

"Just like it was obvious he thinks your therapist is a sadist?"

"That's right."

"You're mistaken." Gabi could have cheered when this time her voice came out casual and offhand, just as she'd intended. "It's true we've become good friends, but nothing more."

A shiver of disloyalty rippled through her at the lie. Why did she feel as if she'd let Jude down by her response?

"Ah, *mija*." Her father expelled a heavy sigh. "Do you think I can't see what's in *your* eyes? On your face? It's clear what you feel for him."

Heat dotted Gabi's cheeks. Was she that transparent? Putting down her fork, she abandoned the pretense of eating. "If there is something between Jude and me—and I'm not saying there is—are you telling me you approve?"

"It depends." Orlando stabbed another bean, looked up. This time his gaze was serious, his lips unsmiling.

"On what?"

"On whether you're willing to be completely honest with him."

Gabi licked her lips. "I don't know what you mean."

"You haven't told him about your transplant."

Something in her father's voice sent a shuddering chill through Gabi. "You didn't tell him." She grabbed her father's arm, her gaze riveted to his. "Tell me you didn't do that."

"He needs to hear it from you," Orlando said mildly, lifting her fingers from his sleeve. "So, no, I didn't mention it."

Releasing a breath, Gabi sagged back in her chair.

"I've never known you to be a coward, Gabriella. I have to say I'm disappointed." Her father's expression might be impassive, but his words held the force of a hard slap.

"I'm not a coward." She lifted her chin. "Jude knows I've had heart surgery. I just haven't decided the best way to tell him what kind."

"Your prognosis is excellent. There's no reason to be afraid." Her father's eyes softened and he reached out to grip her hand. "The man is in love with you. He has a right to know something that's such an important part of your life. Not telling him is tantamount to lying."

"I—" Gabi hesitated.

"Tell him." Her father's tone brooked no argument. "Or I will."

Jude jumped out of his truck in front of Gabi's house, a bouquet of flowers in one hand, a package of steaks in the other and hope in his heart. When he'd visited Orlando earlier today, it sounded as if the man would be released any day. Which meant Jude had to step up his game.

Not that securing Gabi's love was a game. It was more of a mission. He loved her so much he couldn't imagine not having her in his life. He didn't want her for a day, or a week or a year. He wanted her to be his wife, to be the mother of his children, to be the woman he grew old with and loved for eternity.

One hurdle had been jumped when Jude had sat down with Orlando after his therapy session. Jude told him he loved Gabi and wanted to marry her. Because Jude suspected Gabi's father was a traditionalist, he'd asked for his blessing.

The older man had gazed into his eyes for a long moment, as if he could see all the way into Jude's soul. Jude had held steady and let him look. He had nothing to hide. His feelings for Gabi were strong and sincere.

In the end, Orlando had said marrying him would be up to his daughter. But if Gabi said yes, they would have his blessing. Jude had ridden a high the rest of the day.

Tonight, he and Gabi planned to grill steaks then take Chico for a long walk. Jude liked it that they didn't have to do something special to have a good time. Some of his favorite moments with her were when they simply sat on the living room sofa in front of a fire and talked. Or strolled hand in hand in the cool night air with a thousand stars twinkling overhead.

He loved it when she placed her hand in his as if trusting him to look out for her. She was his woman, and he would do everything he could to protect her. To make her happy. And he would love her with each breath until the day he died.

"Jude. Wait up."

He turned to see Alma Peatry striding down the sidewalk toward him, her perfectly groomed standard-size white poodle trotting beside her.

As the gray-haired woman drew close, Jude saw her pale blue eyes snap with undisguised interest. "Flowers and candy. You went all out tonight."

"Actually—" Jude shifted from one boot to the other and lifted the package wrapped in butcher's paper "—these are steaks, not candy."

Her wrinkled face brightened. "T-bones?"

"What else?"

"You devil." Alma's hot-pink painted lips widened. "You'll have the girl eating out of your hands."

"The girl" appeared on the front porch. Gabi's smile flickered for a second when she saw him speaking with Alma, but she hurried over to them. "Hello, Mrs. Peatry."

"It's Alma, dear. Just Alma."

"Taking Monique for a walk, I see." Gabi leaned over and patted the poodle's topknot, while inside the house Chico yapped, obviously not pleased at being left out of the action.

"It's too beautiful of a day to stay inside." Alma glanced down at the poodle. "Ready to rock and roll, Monique?"

The dog gave a high-pitched bark and did a little shimmy. Alma chuckled. "That's affirmative."

Waving a hand carelessly in the air, the woman sauntered down the sidewalk.

"I come bearing three gifts." Jude held out the daisies. "These are for you."

"You brought me daisies the night we ate at The Grill." Pleasure lit Gabi's face. "Thank you. Very much."

"You're very welcome."

She glanced down at his other hand. "Is that my second gift?"

He nodded and held up the package. "Prime beef. Alma assured me steaks are better than candy."

"Definitely." She leaned forward and kissed him lightly on the mouth. "But being with you is the best gift of all."

Though Jude knew they'd agreed to limit public displays of affection, he couldn't resist drawing her to him for a long kiss. "We're on the same wavelength there."

She laughed, a little breathless now, and he followed her inside.

Chico sprang the instant Jude stepped across the threshold. As if on a trampoline, the dog bounced high in the air, making little yipping noises.

Jude grinned. "Looks like you're not the only one who's happy to see me."

"Believe me. You're definitely a bright spot in a dismal day."

Not just the words but something in her tone made Jude stop petting Chico and straighten.

"Papi—" Gabi stopped, shook her head. "Actually, although my father was in a foul mood when I got there, he'd mellowed considerably by the time I left."

Jude watched her intently, now seeing the emotion she'd done such a good job of hiding. He folded her into his arms, pressing her resistant body against him.

"Tell me why you're sad," he whispered against her hair.

She pushed back, raked fingers through her hair. "It's noth—"

"Don't say it's nothing." He kept his tone gentle but firm. "Tell me."

She drew in a deep breath then let it out slowly. "This afternoon I got a call from Rosemary. She's my assistant at the bank. She had distressing news."

"They fired you?"

"No." Gabi gave a nervous laugh. "Although I almost wish that was the news."

Jude took Gabi's ice-cold fingers in his hand and led her to the sofa.

"Rosemary called to tell me about Faith's husband—" Gabi spoke in a scratchy voice, thick with emotion.

While the names were unfamiliar to him, these were obviously people who meant a lot to her. "Faith is—"

"One of my best friends. We work together at the bank. She and Daniel just celebrated their third anniversary. I was maid of honor at their wedding." The words rushed out then abruptly stopped. She cleared her throat before continuing. "Now he's gone."

Gabi's face crumpled and tears welled in her eyes.

"He left her?"

"No. Dear God, no." Gabi wrapped her arms around herself as if freezing. "He was killed."

"What happened?" Jude kept his voice soft and low.

"I thought Faith would have called me, but Rosemary said she was a mess. They were so much in love." Gabi looked at him, her eyes bleak. "She hasn't even returned to work yet. I think Rose said she was coming back in the next few days."

Jude took her hand again, squeezed in a wordless gesture of support.

"Daniel was in Manhattan on business. Apparently he was distracted while crossing a street and didn't notice the light had changed." A shadow crossed her face. "A cab hit him. He—he never regained consciousness."

"Oh, baby." Jude wrapped his arms around her. "When's the funeral? I'll go with you."

The stricken look in her eyes ratcheted up his concern.

"It was weeks ago. He died not long after I left to come here." The words stumbled from her lips in little bursts. "Rosemary didn't want me to feel obligated to come."

"She kept it from you." Because this was her friend and he could see she was upset, Jude tried to keep the condemnation from his voice. It was hard. Her assistant had effectively taken the decision to attend the funeral out of her hands.

Gabi lifted her gaze, a look of bewilderment in her eyes. "Rose knew what Faith and Daniel meant to me. It's not right she took away my choice."

"No," he agreed. "It wasn't right."

"I wish I could have been there." Tears slipped down her cheeks. "I would have been there."

Jude tightened his hold on her, gently stroking her back as she cried. After a moment, she straightened with a sound that was half sob, half laugh.

Chico had climbed up onto the back of the sofa and was leaning over trying to kiss Gabi's tears away.

"Chico, down." He reached for the wiggling dog, who only skittered to the other side of the sofa with the agility of a circus performer.

"Let him be. He's just being my friend." Gabi sniffled and swiped at the remnants of her tears with her fingers. "I'm sorry for unloading on you."

"Hey, goes with the territory." Jude deliberately lightened his tone. "I'm your steady guy, remember?"

A reluctant smile lifted her lips. "Yes, you are."

"That brings us to gift number three." He

reached into his pocket then pressed a ring into her palm. "Now it's official. You and I are going steady."

When Gabi only stared, Jude's heartbeat galvanized. The words tumbled out. "My senior year in high school, our football team took the state championship in our division. First time ever. They had rings made for everyone on the team."

He kissed her forehead. *Keep it light,* he told himself, *Don't spook her.* "I'd like you to have it."

"I can't accept this." She attempted to push the ring into his hands, but Jude shook his head.

"Do you want to date anyone else?" he asked her.

"No, but—"

"I don't, either." He smiled, brushed a tear-soaked tendril of hair back from her cheek. "Jude and Gabi are going steady. She has his ring."

Saying the words in a singsong tone made him feel silly but had the desired effect of bringing a momentary smile back to her lips.

"I'll keep it," she said finally. "For now. But when I leave town, you're taking it back."

Jude wasn't worried. There was no way he was letting her go. And, by the time he got through romancing her, no way she'd want to leave.

"Understood." To seal the deal, Jude kissed her, softly and with great tenderness.

The fear that had been a tight fist around his heart eased. So far, so good.

He'd gotten her to accept one ring from him. Before long, she'd accept another.

Chapter 15

Chapter 15

Shortly before noon, Gabi pulled the Buick into
the lane leading to Deke and Jeanne Marie's
house. When Jude's mother learned Orlando had
been discharged from the rehab center, she'd
called and invited them both over for Sunday
brunch.

Even though he hadn't been home twenty-four
hours, Orlando was determined to attend, especially once he heard Sawyer and Laurel would
be there.

"Are you sure you're up to this, Papi?" Gabi
asked for what felt like the hundredth time. But,
darn it, she didn't like seeing him push himself
so soon after getting home.

"It's lunch," Orlando reminded her cheerfully. "Not a daylong party."

Since he seemed to have no qualms about his ability to handle the outing, Gabi decided to quit questioning the decision. She had to admit his spirits had improved since he'd gotten home. He hadn't voiced a single complaint.

Chico had welcomed him at the door. Despite Orlando's initial resistance, Gabi hadn't been surprised by how quickly he'd taken to the small dog.

The second Orlando had settled into his favorite recliner to watch a basketball game, Chico had jumped onto his lap. With brown eyes firmly fixed on the television, the dorkie had appeared as mesmerized by the action as her father.

With nothing better to do—she'd told Jude she couldn't see him that evening—Gabi had taken a seat on the sofa, prepared to watch two NBA powerhouse teams duke it out on the court. But she found it difficult to focus. All she could think about was Jude and how her best-laid plans had gone awry.

After her conversation with her father at the rehab center on Friday, she'd planned to tell Jude about her transplant. A carefully prepared speech—complete with statistics—had been firmly fixed in her head. Then Rosemary had called.

Everything after that conversation was pretty much a blur. Jude had arrived. Somehow she'd ended up accepting a "going steady" ring from him. A ring that now hung on a chain around her neck.

A fact which made her feel like a lovestruck teen. But she wasn't ready to give it back. Not yet.

Easing the Buick to a stop in front of the house, Gabi's lips lifted in a rueful smile.

"There's the welcoming committee," her father announced.

Gabi glanced over and saw Jude step out of the house, looking yummy enough to eat in slim-cut wool pants, a checked shirt and tailored jacket. She suddenly felt like a country mouse in her chinos and spice-colored cardigan.

But when he smiled at her, every worry disappeared.

Stepping from the car, Gabi lifted a hand in a casual gesture of greeting. But she couldn't stop her smile from blossoming when he hurried toward her.

Orlando chuckled. "Someone is mighty eager to see you."

"I'm sure he just wants to make you feel welcome," Gabi said, even as she moved around the front of the car to close the distance between them.

"Yeah," she heard her father say, "I'm sure that's it."

"Hi," she said, feeling oddly breathless.

"You look beautiful." Jude surprised her by putting his hands on her shoulders and kissing her softly on the lips. With one finger he stroked back a strand of hair that had fallen over her forehead. "I missed you, darlin'. A whole bunch."

"I missed you, too," she whispered back.

Gabi felt heat climb up her neck, knowing her father watched from the front seat. But she was glad Jude seemed to have missed her as much as she'd missed him. Twenty-four hours apart had felt like an eternity.

"I need to get the walker out of the trunk," she said, but couldn't bring herself to step away from him.

"I'll take care of it." With obvious reluctance, Jude dropped his hands from her shoulders. He opened her father's door as he made his way to the back of the car to retrieve the walker. "Good to see you, Mr. Mendoza."

"Call me Orlando." A half smile played at the corners of her father's lips. "After all, we're practically family."

Family? Gabi frowned. *Where had that come from?*

"How was your first night at home... Orlando?" Keeping a firm grip on her father's arm, Jude helped the older man to his feet.

Orlando steadied himself, which Gabi could see by the tension on his face was no easy task. "Nothing beats sleeping in your own bed. I expected you to stop by. Say hello."

Jude shot a glance at Gabi. "I thought you might need time to settle in."

"I was tired," Orlando admitted. "More than I thought I'd be. But my Gabriella is an angel. She made sure I had everything I needed."

"Oh, Papi," Gabi protested. "I didn't do anything."

"You made that delicious meal for supper," Orlando insisted. "What did you call it? Rush Hour Something?"

"Rush Hour Stew," Gabi murmured.

Jude's eyes met hers. He smiled. "I wish I'd been there. It's a favorite of mine."

"Next time." Orlando grunted and wheeled the walker up the walk, halting every few feet.

Gabi kept to the left side of her father while Jude took the right side as Orlando inched his way to the front door.

Even though spring hadn't fully arrived, large pots of flowers decorated the front of the house. When Jude opened the door, the delicious scent of sizzling bacon and sausage teased

Gabi's nostrils while the din of conversation assailed her ears.

There were people everywhere. Adults laughed and talked in the parlor. Several children Gabi didn't recognize ran through the house. Jude's sister Stacey caught her eye and offered a friendly wave. The blonde stood, baby Piper in her arms, chatting animatedly with Sawyer and Laurel.

"Welcome. Welcome." Jeanne Marie appeared in the foyer, arms opened wide in greeting.

Jude's mother wore a long, flowing turquoise skirt and a blouse with turquoise and silver threads running through the fabric. Large dangly earrings with a Southwestern design hung from her ears, a matching necklace on her throat.

"Orlando, it's so good to see you up and walking." She led them to the parlor and motioned for her daughter Delaney to get up from where she was sitting. "I've just the spot for you."

"I don't want to take the young lady's chair," Orlando protested, shooting Delaney an apologetic look.

"You aren't, Mr. Mendoza," Delaney assured him, her pretty face earnest. "I need to help Mom get the food on the table."

"If you're sure," he said, even as he aimed the walker toward the chair.

"Positive." Delaney glanced at her mother. "I'll fill the water glasses with ice."

Jeanne Marie gave Delaney an approving smile. "Thanks, honey."

Once her father reached the chair, it took a little maneuvering to get him settled with his booted leg propped on an ottoman.

"Orlando." Sawyer's deep voice called out as he and his wife, Laurel, hurried over. "You look better every time I see you."

"That tells me I must have looked pretty bad before." Her father's words made Sawyer and Laurel laugh.

Gabi rolled her eyes even as contentment draped like a warm blanket around her shoulders. Papi had to be feeling good to joke.

While Orlando spoke with the couple about the NTSB investigation into the crash, Gabi caught Jeanne Marie's arm.

"Is there any way my father could be seated at the end of the table?" Gabi kept her voice low. "I'm sorry to make special demands when we're guests, but I think it would be easier—"

"Not a problem, my dear." Jeanne Marie gave Gabi's arm a reassuring squeeze. "I'm having the food set up buffet-style. Everyone can fill their plate and sit wherever they like. Your father won't need to move from where he is now. I have TV trays available for those eating in the parlor."

"We'll eat with Orlando," Jude told his mother, positioning himself next to Gabi. "I'm betting Sawyer and Laurel will, also."

It was an excellent solution. Gabi wondered if Jeanne Marie chose to serve lunch in this manner because of her father's limited mobility.

As if she could read her mind, Jude's mother put an arm around Gabi's shoulder. "In this community we take care of our own. Your father is one of us now."

"Thank you." Gabi swallowed hard past the sudden lump in her throat. "Knowing he's among friends means so much."

Even as she fought for control, tears stung the backs of Gabi's eyes. Her father had hit the jackpot when he'd moved to this little town in Northern Texas. He had a job he loved and people who cared about him. The only thing that would make him happier was if his children all lived nearby.

"I'll be back in a few minutes." Jeanne Marie gave Gabi's arm a squeeze. "From the look I'm getting from my daughter, I'm needed in the kitchen."

"Your mother is nice," Gabi told Jude as Jeanne Marie scurried off.

"She likes you." His eyes were clear and very blue. "A lot."

Gabi looked at him doubtfully. "I wouldn't

think she knows me well enough to form an opinion."

"She knows what I tell her." Jude's hand grazed the bare skin above her blouse. "It's all good."

The simple brush of his fingers against her neck sent a shiver of longing rushing through her.

His expression softened as he gazed down at her. For a second Gabi thought he might kiss her. Right there in the midst of all his family. And she might have let him. But when two of his brothers who were walking by stopped, Jude stepped back.

Though Chris stayed but a second, barely long enough to say hello, Liam appeared in no particular hurry. He settled his blue eyes on Gabi. "You've been keeping my little brother busy."

Gabi slanted a sideways glance at Jude and smiled. "You could say he's been my personal tour guide to all things Horseback Hollow."

"He's not going to know what to do with all his free time once you're gone," Liam joked.

"Shut up, Liam," Jude said mildly.

Liam grinned and ignored him, keeping his focus on Gabi. "Any idea when you'll head back to Miami?"

Sensing Jude's scrutiny, Gabi chose her words carefully. "I have a woman starting tomorrow who'll cook, clean and do laundry for my father. A physical therapist and home health nurse will also be stopping by regularly. I won't be leaving until I'm confident his needs are well covered."

Once Liam walked off, Jude turned to her. "I didn't realize you had all those plans in place."

"My father insisted we do a lot of preplanning. He's worried about my job." At least he had been, Gabi thought, before his recent change of heart. "Even though my leave was approved, he's convinced they're going to put someone else in my position and give me the boot."

"Would that be such a bad thing?"

Startled, she blinked.

"You could apply for the position Steve mentioned." Jude took her hand, linked her fingers with his. "That way you could be around to personally supervise your father's recovery."

"My life is in Miami," she murmured, her mouth suddenly dry as sand.

"It *was* in Miami." Jude brought her hand to his lips and pressed a kiss into the palm. "What I'm trying to say is—"

His head jerked up as the sound of loud voices coming from the foyer drew his attention.

"What do you mean you're moving to Red Rock?" Anger filled Deke's voice. "I was counting on you this spring. You know this is our busiest season."

"Calving. Branding. Putting up hay. Grunt work," Chris declared in a derisive tone. "I have a brain. I'd like to use it for a change. Working for the Fortunes will give me that opportunity."

"You think you're too good to work with your hands? Is that it?"

Gabi wasn't sure if everyone heard the faint undercurrent of hurt in Deke's voice, but she caught it. Perhaps it was because her headstrong father was a lot like Deke Jones. She'd witnessed the anger and the hurt feelings that resulted when he and her brothers had butted heads.

"Let's just say I'm too smart to continue wasting my life on some two-bit ranch." Chris spoke in that smart-alecky tone guaranteed to light a father's fuse.

The clack of boots on hardwood echoed as Deke followed Chris onto the porch. Now that they were outside, Gabi had a perfect view of the two men through the window.

Fortunately the raised voices couldn't be heard over the noisy conversations in the living room.

"Don't walk away from me, boy." Deke's voice lashed sharp as a whip.

Chris stopped, turned back toward his father. The set of his face was rigid, austere, as if it had been carved from granite. Except for the sneer on his lips, which made his handsome face ugly.

"Let's face it. You never understood me. And

I sure as hell never understood you. Why anyone would want to waste his life tending cattle is beyond me." Chris gave a humorless laugh. "The Fortunes could buy everything you own, down to that prizewinning bull you're so proud of, out of petty cash."

The words shot from Chris's lips like bullets. Gabi had no doubt they were intended to wound the target. By the rage building on Deke's face, they'd hit the mark square on.

"They run big businesses," Chris continued. "Important businesses. They command power and respect."

"Good for them." Deke spat the words. "But you seem to be forgetting one important fact. You're not a Fortune. You're Chris Jones."

"Christopher *Fortune* Jones," Chris responded with extra emphasis. "I'm going to make something of myself."

"This has gone on long enough." Jude's easy smile had disappeared. He was clenching his jaw tight, and his hands were now fisted at his sides. But when he started to move, his mother stepped forward and grabbed his arm.

"Let your father handle this," she told her son in a low tone. "This is between him and Chris. You don't need to be getting in the middle of it."

"He's gone too far this time," Jude argued. "Acting like Dad is nothing and the Fortunes—"

"Jude." His mother's grip tightened. "I said let your father handle this."

"—and I'm not coming back."

Gabi shifted her attention just in time to see Chris hop into a pickup, slam the door shut and tear off down the road in a cloud of dust.

Standing as tall and stiff as any statue, Deke watched him drive off.

"Reminds me of some of the arguments between my father and brothers." Gabi kept her tone light, hoping to defuse some of the tension.

"Chris and his daddy." Jeanne Marie gave a little laugh, though her eyes remained troubled. "Oil and water."

Before Gabi could even begin to formulate a response, Jeanne Marie turned toward the roomful of family and friends and clapped her hands. The chatter of voices immediately ceased.

"It's time to eat." The older woman's gaze shifted to Orlando. She smiled. "Before we start, I'd like a round of applause for our guest. Orlando Mendoza is back home and racing down the road to a full recovery. Orlando, we couldn't be happier."

Her father blushed as everyone applauded and cheered.

By the time Gabi got her food and settled down next to Jude on the sofa, her mind had already made several trips back to her earlier conversation with Jude. She had the feeling he'd been about to ask her to stay.

It was probably best he'd been interrupted by his brothers. She still had to tell him about the transplant. Lay it all out. The good. The bad. The ugly.

She'd thought she could just walk away. But her need for him, her *love* for him, was a powerful force, urging her to discuss the matter with him before making any decisions. Just in case she was wrong and having a family wasn't that important to him.

Yes, she would tell him. Then they would see.

The dishes had been cleared and she'd risen to grab some dessert for her father when a sweet-smelling baby in a candy-striped dress with a pink headband was thrust into her arms.

"Could you hold Piper a sec, Gabi?" Stacey danced from one foot to the other. "Delaney and I have been on this drinking-more-water kick. The downside is now I have to pee every five minutes."

"Sure."

The word had barely made it past Gabi's lips when Stacey dashed off, leaving a seven-month-old who smelled like talcum powder in her arms. Piper gazed up, her green eyes large and luminous. For a second, Gabi feared she'd cry, but then the baby's rosebud of a mouth blossomed into a smile.

"You're such a cutie," Gabi crooned. She felt a lovely ache that went all the way down to her soul when the baby gurgled and waved her plump arms. "And this pink headband with the bling is super stylish."

"Reminds me of her at that age," Gabi heard her father say. "Prettiest little thing you ever saw."

Gabi looked up and realized she had an audience.

Her dad's eyes were dark with memories that likely included her mother. But it was the expression of longing and love she saw on Jude's face that ripped her in two. She knew his face, understood in that moment he was seeing her holding his child, *their* child, and envisioning a long and happy life with her by his side.

Suddenly the baby felt unspeakably heavy in her arms and the ring she wore beneath her sweater hung like a millstone around her neck. Thankfully, Stacey soon breezed back into the room to take the child.

While her father and Jude enjoyed the dessert of peach cobbler, Gabi brooded. She should have stuck to her original plan and kept things easy-breezy between her and Jude. She never should have let herself fall in love with him.

At least she'd come to her senses in time. She couldn't guarantee Jude the babies he wanted or a long life with the woman he loved. No matter what he might say, he wanted those things. The truth had been in his eyes.

That's why as soon as Gabi saw her father settled, she would leave Horseback Hollow and Jude Fortune Jones. Because she loved him, because she wanted the best for him, she had no choice.

Chapter 16

Jude hated that he felt resentful of Orlando's improved health, but it was hard not to, considering he'd barely had a second alone with Gabi since her father had been released from the rehab center.

After lunch on Sunday, he'd offered to ride home with Gabi and help Orlando get settled. But Gabi had put him off, telling him she wanted some dad-and-daughter time.

On Monday when he called she'd said the nurse, therapist, as well as Orlando's new health aide would be in and out all day so she didn't want more company.

Jude told her he understood, but he didn't. He wasn't *company*. But he hadn't argued. She'd sounded tired and stressed, and he'd begun to wonder if her father's care was turning out to be more than she'd anticipated. Perhaps more than she could handle.

Thankfully today had started on an upswing. Orlando had texted him at the crack of dawn, sounding upbeat and cheerful. Gabi had called and asked him to come over at four.

The invitation gave him hope things were leveling off and they were settling into a routine. Frankly, he'd been worried about her.

When she left the ranch house on Sunday, the lines of strain that had appeared on her face as the afternoon progressed had been the only reason he hadn't followed through with his plan of enticing her out to the pond and getting down on one knee.

As he parked his truck in front of Orlando's house, he saw Alma standing on her curb, sweeping the street. Monique sat like a princess in the yard, tall and regal, watching her mistress work.

Jude waved.

"It's good to have Orlando home," she called out.

He deserved an Academy Award for his enthusiastic agreement.

Gabi opened the door to his knock. "Jude."

"You remember my name," he said in a teasing tone, then gave her a quick kiss before pushing past her to step inside. "It's a good start."

Pulling the door shut behind him, she brought a hand to her lips, looking oddly flustered. She wore jeans, sneakers and a long-sleeved blue Henley. Her hair was pulled back in a low ponytail. The shadows under her eyes and her paleness were new and made him frown.

It wasn't simply the pallor that concerned him; it was the sadness in her eyes. But when he reached for her hand, she stepped away with a casualness that seemed too calculated to be anything but deliberate.

Unease slithered up his spine.

"Who is it?" Orlando yelled over the television noise.

"It's Jude," Gabi announced as she followed him into the room.

Orlando looked up from where he was positioned in front of a big screen tuned to a sitcom popular in the late eighties.

"Hey, Jude," her father said, then chuckled as if he'd made an original joke. "It's good to see you. Gabi mentioned you'd be dropping by."

"It's such a beautiful day, I thought I might entice your daughter to play hooky and take a short walk with me." Jude shifted his gaze to Gabi, offered what he hoped was an engaging smile. "Chico, too."

The dog, currently sitting on Orlando's lap, lifted his head and began to whine softly.

"I don't think I should go that f—" Gabi began.

"There's a park just around the corner," Jude said before she could refuse. "With swings."

"Gabi loves to swing," Orlando said.

She cast her father a narrowed, glinting glance.

"Well, you do." The older man shrugged, a smile tipping his lips.

"It's settled." Jude gave a short whistle and Chico jumped down and came to him.

"I couldn't possibly leave my father alone." Gabi spoke so quickly she stumbled over the words. "He just got home a few days ago."

"I'm more than capable of watching television without a nursemaid hovering—" Orlando paused, reached over and took his daughter's hand at the stricken look on her face. "Don't get me wrong. I love having you with me, fussing and making sure I have what I need. But you and Chico should take a walk with Jude. It'll do you both good to get out of the house, breathe some fresh air."

"Okay," she said finally, reluctantly, then leaned over to kiss her father's cheek. "I won't be long."

"Take your time." Orlando waved his good hand in the air. "My show is just starting."

"Do you need anything before I go?" Gabi asked.

"I'm fine."

"Your cell phone is right there." Gabi pointed to a tray table next to her father's chair. "I'm taking mine with me. If you need anything, call."

"Go." Orlando waved her away without shifting his eyes from the screen.

Bright patches of pink stained Gabi's cheeks. She grabbed a leash and clipped it onto Chico's collar. When she reached the door, Gabi hesitated once more. But after seeing her father's gaze still glued to the television, she stepped outside without another word.

Wanting to comfort, Jude placed a palm at the small of her back, but her instant recoil had him dropping his hand to his side.

As they walked, Chico trotted happily between them.

"Nice evening," Gabi said in the polite tone you'd use with a stranger.

"It is indeed." Jude turned at the corner in the direction of the small park.

He'd hoped she would voluntarily share what was troubling her. But when another block passed in silence, Jude decided to go with the direct approach. "Tell me what's going on, Gabi. I want to help."

A nervous laugh slipped past her lips. "I don't know what you mean."

"For starters, you've been freezing me out." He slanted a sideways glance. "Did I do something on Sunday to offend you? Is that why I've been banished to Siberia?"

"No," she said quickly. *Too quickly.* "Of course not."

Jude waited for her to continue.

"You didn't do anything other than maybe put the wrong spin on things." She licked her lips. "That's why I asked you to come over, to set things straight."

A knot twisted in the pit of his stomach.

"I mean, what we had was supposed to be fun, but that's all." She huffed out a breath. "On Sunday I got the feeling you wanted more."

He did want more. Marriage. Kids. As his father would say, the whole ball of wax. She wanted that, too.

Before he could respond, she pulled his championship ring out from beneath her shirt and jerked the chain up and over her head. When she pressed the ring into his hand, he took it only to casually cast it into the cavernous depths of the bag slung over her shoulder.

Her lips pressed together. "I don't want to go steady anymore."

"I don't, either."

The response, delivered in a matter-of-fact tone, caught her off guard.

"You don't?" For a second her eyes widened. "I mean that's good. We're in agreement. Let me give this back to—"

She started to reach into the bag, but Jude laid a restraining hand on her arm. "I don't want to go steady with you," he said softly. "I want to marry you."

Gabi yanked back with such force she'd have fallen if he hadn't reached out to steady her.

"You don't want to marry me," she insisted, panic in her voice.

"I do."

"You don't know me." Frustration ground through her words like shards of glass.

Something was going on. Jude was sure of it. And whatever it was didn't have a darn thing to do with her father. He wished he could simply kiss the problem away. But he had a feeling this one was like a splinter. It would need to be dug out before they could be done with it and move on.

"I do know you." He gentled his tone, recognizing her increasing distress even if he didn't understand the reason for it yet. "Quite well, in fact."

They reached the playground. While the newer section, with its play center of slides and decks was overrun with toddlers, the area holding the swings was deserted. Jude took a seat in one of the slings and motioned for Gabi to take the one beside him. Chico sprawled in the sand at her feet and stared longingly at the children playing.

"You *think* you know me, but you don't." She slipped the band from her head and gave her hair a toss.

"I know everything important."

"Did you know I had a heart transplant when I was nineteen?" Gabi knew she wasn't playing fair, but she saw no choice. His future happiness had to be her primary concern.

Jude brought his swing, which had been swaying ever-so-slightly, to an abrupt halt. "What?"

She met his startled gaze head-on. "I had a heart transplant. Seven years ago."

For a second Jude forgot how to breathe. "You said you had heart surgery."

"A heart transplant is heart surgery," she said in a disdainful tone.

Jude didn't know much about transplants other than they were a big deal. And usually, like Leslie, who was now recovering in Houston from a liver transplant, you had to be pretty ill before getting one. He leveled a long stare in her direction. "Why did you have one?"

Surprisingly, she gave him the details without much prompting. He listened as she recounted the bout of stomach flu, the shortness of breath, learning the virus from the gastroenteritis had attacked the heart and left it with irreversible damage.

His blood ran cold at the thought of how close she'd come to losing her life.

"That's why I'm so focused on eating healthy and exercising," she added.

"Makes sense," Jude said automatically, even though right now nothing was making sense.

He felt as if he'd plunged into an alternate world. The way Gabi was acting didn't make sense. The fact that she'd kept something that was such an important part of her life a secret from him sure as heck didn't make sense. "Why didn't you tell me before now?"

"Our relationship was supposed to be light— just fun and games." She lifted one shoulder in the type of irritating shrug his sisters often used. "Heart transplant stuff is heavy."

His head spun. Forget alternate world. He'd fallen headlong into an alternate universe. "Then *why* tell me now?"

"Because you seem to have gotten the mistaken impression there's more depth to our relationship than actually exists." Her tone was cool, distant. "I used the disclosure of the transplant to illustrate you don't know me as well as you think."

Jude fought his way through the fog shrouding his brain.

"On Sunday, you told me how much you missed me." *That* he knew he hadn't misunderstood. In fact, his heart warmed now remembering her words and the intense emotion he'd seen in her eyes.

Gabi hesitated only a second.

"It was code." Her laugh reminded him of nails on a chalkboard. "I was telling you I missed having sex with you."

"You seriously expect me to believe I meant nothing to you? That what existed between us was only about good sex?"

Something flickered in those dark depths before a shutter dropped, hiding any emotion.

"That's exactly right." Hopping off her swing, Gabi tugged on Chico's leash then shot Jude a bright smile. "I should get back to my father. I'm glad we had a chance to clear this up before I left."

He pressed fingers against his temples, where a headache had begun to pound, making it difficult to think. "When are you leaving?"

"Does it matter?" She tilted her head, her brown eyes unreadable. "With my dad home, there can't be any more between-the-sheets action."

Jude could only stare. Could he really have been so wrong about…everything?

The walk back from the park was a blur, and when they reached the house, Jude didn't come in. Gabi didn't really expect him to and told herself she was glad he'd gotten the message.

Keeping that phony smile on her face all the way home when all she wanted to do was dissolve into tears had taken all her energy. She wasn't sure how much longer she'd have been able to keep up the pretense he meant nothing to her.

She stepped inside the house, conscious of a truck door slamming shut, then seconds later, an engine roaring to life and tires squealing.

Still, Gabi didn't let her guard down until the front door was firmly shut behind her and locked. Only then did she allow the tears to fall.

"How was the walk?" her father called out. "Is Jude still with you?"

Gabi unclipped Chico's leash then hurriedly swiped the tears from her cheeks.

"He had to get back to the ranch." She forced a bright smile and strolled into the living room.

"You were right. It was nice to get some fresh air. And Chico really enjoyed the park. There were a lot of kids there and he couldn't take his eyes off of them."

With sudden horror, Gabi realized she was babbling. She clamped her mouth shut. At least she'd done a stellar job of keeping her tone light, or so she thought, until her father's gaze latched on to hers.

"What's wrong?" he demanded.

You mean other than me decimating the man I love with a pack of lies?

"No-nothing."

Orlando's gaze narrowed. "Did that boy say something to upset you?"

"Actually, I believe I may have upset him." Gabi fought to project a cavalier tone. "I told him, because I'd soon be heading back to Miami, I didn't see any reason for us to continue our friendship."

"Friendship."

Gabi nodded. "That's right."

A watchful look filled her father's eyes. The same look she'd seen numerous times in high school when she slipped in past curfew and tried to fib about it the next morning.

He always seemed to be able to tell when she was stretching the truth. In fact, he'd once told her he could even tell when she was lying to herself.

Gabi settled herself on the sofa, forced herself to breathe past the tightness in her chest. "Oh, and you'll be happy to know, I told him about the transplant."

Orlando's dark eyes flickered but his expression remained impassive. "How did he react?"

"He asked why. I told him. He was surprised I hadn't told him before." Her tone turned clipped as she fought to keep her emotions under control. "Ah, well, it was fun while it lasted."

"He's in love with you."

Gabi started to deny it then shrugged. "Maybe."

"You're in love with him."

Gabi shifted her gaze to the silly sitcom playing on the television. The characters acted as if life was one big joke. Maybe it was for some, but not for her. Gabi jerked her head toward the screen. "Mind if I turn it off?"

Orlando picked up the remote, flicked off the television, then turned back to his daughter. "I can't believe Jude doesn't want to be with you because you've had a heart transplant."

Her father's voice was heavy with disappointment.

"It wasn't him. I'm the one who said it was over between us." Gabi paced a moment then returned to sit. "He wanted to get serious. Since I don't plan to marry, I didn't see the point in continuing a relationship with him."

"Even though you love him you don't want to marry him?" Now her father looked totally confused.

"I don't want to marry *anyone*. I saw what you went through with Mama." Gabi wiped her sweaty palms on her jeans and did her best to control the tremble that kept trying to creep into her voice. "I have a new heart, Papi. But we both know there are no guarantees I'll stay healthy. My body could reject it tomorrow."

Her father's eyes softened. "There are no guarantees with anything in life, *mija*."

"Some women are better bets than others." She rested her head against the back of the chair. "I won't put Jude through the pain of losing a wife. You, of all people, should understand that by walking away I'm giving him a gift."

"I understand love and wanting to protect." Orlando stared into her troubled face. "But every day I had with your mother was precious."

Gabi simply shrugged

"He won't give up," Orlando warned. "He loves you too much to just walk away."

"Then I'll just have to do or say whatever necessary to get him to stop loving me," she said in a weary voice. "I'm sure he's already rethinking how he feels about me after our conversation this afternoon."

As Orlando gazed at the face of his only daughter, he realized she needed time and distance to clearly consider all she was giving up by charting this course. She was smart, his Gabriella. He believed she'd soon see that Jude had a right to be a part of a decision that affected his future.

In the meantime, he couldn't sit by and let her destroy Jude's love. Not when he knew the cowboy would make such a fine husband and son-in-law.

"Gabriella," he said, "I believe it's time for you to return to Miami."

"Soon," Gabi agreed. "After I make sure you have everything you need then—"

"Between the woman you've hired and my nurse and therapist, I'm covered. You need to get back to your job and your life in Miami." His tone brooked no argument.

"You're right." Gabi sighed and glanced at the dog on his lap. "But I'm going to need a favor. Could you possibly watch Chico until I find a place that allows dogs?"

Gabi shifted under the animal's unyielding stare and remembered promising him he'd always be with her. But it couldn't be helped. Just like walking away from Jude, that couldn't be helped, either.

"Of course he can stay with me." Orlando scrubbed the top of the dog's head with his knuckles. "I've grown fond of the little guy."

Gabi clumsily pulled herself upright. It felt as if everything was suddenly moving at warp speed. Which was good, she told herself. Once a decision was made, you went with it. "I'll have to start checking for flights—"

"I have a friend who's a bigwig at one of the airlines that fly out of Lubbock. I'll call him tonight. He owes me a favor. We may be able to work something out for tomorrow."

"Tomorrow?" Gabi gaped. "You must really want to get rid of me."

Though she tried to keep the hurt from her voice, she wasn't entirely successful.

"Ah, *mija*." He held out a hand to her, wrapping his fingers tightly around hers when she came to him. "I love you. While it's been wonderful having you here, it's time for you to go. Trust me, this is for the best."

His gaze dropped to their interlocked hands.

"I have to admit when you came I hoped you'd love it so much you'd want to make it your home, too," he said softly. "I'm sorry that didn't happen. Sorry things didn't work out."

She knew what he was saying. Her father

had hoped she'd stay in Horseback Hollow and marry Jude. He liked her cowboy, she realized suddenly. Liked him a lot. Instead of comforting her, the knowledge only added to her pain.

"I'm sorry, too, Papi." She brought his hand to her cheek, resting the side of her face against his large workman's hands. "So very sorry."

Chapter 17

Bright and early Wednesday morning, while the home health nurse was busy with her father, Gabi packed for her afternoon flight. She was headed to the kitchen for some Ziploc bags when the doorbell sounded.

"I'll get it," she called out, detouring to the front of the house.

Right before her hand closed over the knob, Gabi had a sudden image of Jude, standing on the porch, daisies in hand, begging her to stay.

When she opened the door it wasn't Jude but his mother who stood on the porch, a bakery box in one hand and a smile that reminded Gabi of the man she was trying so hard to forget.

"Jeanne Marie, how nice of you to drop by."

Though seeing the woman tugged at her heartstrings, Gabi smiled warmly. "I'm afraid my father isn't available right now. The nurse just got here."

"Actually, it's you I came to see." Jeanne Marie raised the box. "Although I did bring enough scones for your father and his caregivers, as well."

"That's very kind." Gabi stepped back. "Would you like to come in? I can make coffee."

"I'd love a cup."

"I hope decaf is okay. It's all we have."

"It's perfect. While you get the coffee started, I can get plates for the scones," Jeanne Marie offered when they reached the tiny kitchen.

"The dishes are in the cupboard to the right of the sink." Gabi started the coffee then set out skim milk and sugar.

The older woman pulled out two plates then placed a scone on each. She turned back to Gabi. "I hope you like cranberry-orange."

Gabi gave a little laugh. "I like them all."

While fruit scones tended to be higher in sugar than the plain kind, Gabi decided she'd make an exception this time and simply enjoy the treat.

"Was that a suitcase I saw in the hall?" Jeanne Marie asked moments later, lifting a mug of steaming coffee to her lips.

"It's mine." Gabi kept her tone matter-of-fact as she broke off a piece of quick bread. "Now that my father is on the mend, it's time for me to head home."

Jeanne Marie's eyes registered surprise. "This seems awfully sudden. You didn't mention anything about leaving when I saw you on Sunday."

Gabi popped a bite of scone into her mouth, forced herself to chew. "The bank will only hold my position for so long."

"Does Jude know you're leaving today?"

Gabi chose her words carefully. "He's aware I planned to return to Miami."

"No wonder he was distraught." Jeanne Marie spoke bluntly, a frown furrowing her brows. "You realize my son is in love with you?"

Gabi wasn't about to negotiate that minefield.

"Jude's been in love before." *Easy-breezy,* she told herself. "No doubt he will be again."

Yet the mere thought of him with another woman brought a searing pain to her chest.

Jeanne Marie snorted. "If you believe that, you're not as bright as I think you are."

Even though the scone had tasted like sawdust in her mouth, Gabi took another bite and kept her expression impassive. If Jeanne Marie hoped to goad her into a reaction, it wasn't happening.

The older woman fixed her steely-blue eyes on Gabi. "You'll break his heart if you leave."

I'll break it if I stay.

For a second Gabi feared she'd spoken her thoughts aloud. But when Jeanne Marie's expression didn't change, Gabi took another bite of scone and washed it down with a big gulp of coffee.

"Deke and I stopped by Jude's place last night." Jeanne Marie pursed her lips. "Even though he staunchly insisted nothing was wrong, I could tell he was lying. A mother knows such things."

Gabi squelched a nervous laugh. Shades of her father. Could it be parents were issued a built-in lie detector when children were born?

"Family means everything to Jude," Gabi said through lips that felt frozen. "And to you."

"We're a close-knit group." Jeanne Marie nodded as if the words required additional emphasis then added. "Most of us, anyway."

The older woman sighed and for a second, a look of profound sadness shadowed her eyes.

It was obvious Jeanne Marie was thinking of Deke and Chris. Though she hid it well, Gabi had seen on Sunday how much the argument between her husband and youngest son troubled her.

"Now you have even more family to love," Gabi pointed out, nudging the conversation in a different direction. "You're part of the Fortune family. Connected by blood."

Jeanne Marie's expression relaxed.

"Becoming acquainted with family I never knew existed has been wonderful. But I love and adore my adoptive parents even though we're not related by blood." Jeanne Marie inclined her head, a quizzical look on her face. "What's this about, Gabi?"

Gabi dropped her hands to her lap so Jeanne Marie wouldn't notice the trembling. "It's my rather awkward attempt to point out that Jude is surrounded by people who love him. And to assure you that you needn't worry. He'll do fine without me in his life."

Was it Jeanne Marie she was trying to assure of that fact? Gabi wondered. Or herself?

Jeanne Marie leaned forward, rested her elbows on the table. "My son is a good man—kind and loving. He'll make a wonderful husband."

The woman was like Chico with a bone. And, while Gabi knew it was unintentional, it felt as if Jeanne Marie had snatched up a butter knife and plunged it straight into her heart.

"I have no doubt Jude will be a good husband." Gabi smiled politely. "But not to me."

Color rose in Jeanne Marie's cheeks, and for the first time since she arrived she appeared embarrassed. "I'm not normally an interfering woman. I certainly wouldn't be one of those stick-my-nose-into-your-business mothers-in-law everyone jokes about. It's just that, though he's doing a good job of hiding it, my son is hurting."

Jeanne Marie brought a work-hardened hand to her floral blouse and placed it on her chest. "Seeing him suffer breaks my heart."

Genuine, loving concern radiated from every pore of the woman's body. For a second, Gabi was seized with the urge to fling herself into Jeanne Marie's arms and beg her to make it all better.

But Gabi wasn't a child. And Jeanne Marie would never be her mother, not even by virtue of marriage. Yet, the desire to do something so radical told Gabi that her control over her emotions hung by a slender thread. If Jeanne Marie mentioned Jude's unhappiness one more time, Gabi might break down and sob.

"I'm sorry I have to cut this short, but I have a plane to catch." Gabi pushed back her chair and stood. "Your family has been so kind to me and my father. I appreciate you stopping by and giving me this opportunity to personally thank you for all you've done."

Jeanne Marie pulled to her feet. Her eyes seemed to soften as they surveyed Gabi's face.

"I'll see you again, my dear." The older woman placed her hand flat against Gabi's cheek. "Very soon."

* * *

Jude dropped down on a bench outside his barn and took a putty knife to his muddy boots. While he scraped, he brooded. Once he'd been able to factor out the emotion, he realized what Gabi had told him had been nothing but a huge scoop of bull.

She loved him. While she may not have said the words, he had eyes. He'd seen the emotion in that big, beautiful, brown-eyed gaze. Yet she'd felt the need to make him believe she didn't care. Why?

He had the feeling the reason had something to do with her heart transplant. It was a logical assumption, considering she'd deliberately withheld that bit of information from him, a fact which had initially pissed him off royally.

But he'd forced himself to put aside the anger and focus on discovering just what was going on in that head of hers. Despite spending much of last night researching heart transplants and hoping something would jump out at him, the root of her rejection remained as muddy as his boots.

He had lots of facts. But no answers.

"I thought you'd be out riding the range."

Jude glanced up to see Sawyer striding across the yard looking very much out of place in his suit and Italian loafers.

"What are you doing way out here?" Jude finished with one boot and began on the other. "I thought you'd be ten thousand feet in the wild blue teaching someone how to crash."

"It's 'how to fly' and that's on tap for later." Sawyer's face eased into a smile as he glanced at Jude's boots. "What did you do to those Tony Lama boots?"

"Cow decided to give birth to twins in the only muddy spot in the whole damn pasture." Jude's lips curved. "Had a little trouble, but Doc Green and I got her a happy ending."

"Congratulations." Sawyer lifted his briefcase. "I brought those papers you wanted. I can leave them in the house."

"I'd appreciate it." Jude rose to his feet. "I need to get some hay to the herd in the north pasture."

He walked with his cousin on his way toward the house.

"What'd you think of Gabi leaving so suddenly?" Sawyer asked casually just as Jude turned to get into his pickup.

When Jude had been nine, Liam had knocked him out of their tree house. He'd hit the ground with a solid thud, hard enough to knock the air from his lungs. Jude remembered how he felt that day. He felt the same way now.

"Left?" Jude was surprised at how rational he

sounded with the chaos inside him. "Where'd she go?"

"Back to Miami." Sawyer shrugged. "Laurel gave her a lift into Lubbock. We were both surprised she was leaving so soon, but Gabi said there wasn't any reason for her to stay in Horseback Hollow any longer."

Jude's fingers tightened into fists. He focused on breathing. In. Out. In. Out. When he finally had his emotions under control, he smiled grimly. "Looks like I'll be taking a little trip to Florida."

"You're going after her?" There was surprise in Sawyer's voice.

"Damn straight." Jude spoke through gritted teeth. "Gabi and I can't get our…situation…resolved with a bunch of miles between us."

Sawyer stared at him thoughtfully. "But if she doesn't want you—"

"Damn it, Sawyer." Jude slammed his hand against the side of the truck, almost relishing the pain that shot up his arm. "She does want me. But something is causing her to back the hell away. I need to dig out what it is and make it right."

A ghost of a smile touched Sawyer's lips. "Well, since you put it that way…any ideas what the 'something' is?"

"No," Jude said immediately then paused as a

sudden image of the longing on Gabi's face when she'd been holding Piper surfaced. "Maybe."

"Good luck." Sawyer clapped a hand on Jude's shoulder. "I hope it works out."

"It will," Jude said, because the only outcome he'd accept was he and Gabi together, forever.

Gabi arrived in Miami late Wednesday night and walked through the bank's employee entrance bright and early the next morning.

There was really no alternative. Unless she wanted to stay in her apartment—which was in the middle of being fumigated—and cry. No, it was best to jump back into her life with both feet.

The trouble was, it didn't feel like her life anymore. Battling the traffic on the drive to the bank made her long for the quiet roadways surrounding Horseback Hollow. Seeing the palm trees lining the boulevard felt...odd. And the humidity. Had it always been this oppressive?

Thankfully, her office was a cool oasis and the work that had piled up in her absence kept her mind busy and off Jude. Or so she tried to convince herself. At two-thirty, she decided to stretch her legs and refill the mug of water she kept on her desk.

At this time of day the break room should be deserted, which was an added bonus. Gabi was sick to death of answering questions about Texas and her father. Her dad was doing well, she assured her coworkers. And she agreed that Texas was far different than Miami. Yes, she had seen cows and had even, gasp, ridden a horse.

The hardest was when they teased her about all the hunky cowboys. She pushed open the break room door, blinking back unexpected tears, reminding herself for the zillionth time that walking away from Jude had been for the best.

Gabi stepped back, startled, when she realized the room wasn't empty. But her disappointment turned to pleasure when she saw it was her friend Faith rising from the table.

"Rose told me you were at an outside meeting today." For the first time since setting foot on Florida soil, Gabi was glad she was back. Though she and Faith had spoken on the phone several times since she'd heard the news of Daniel's death, it wasn't the same as being here with her.

"I'm so glad to see you." Emotion clogged Gabi's throat as she crossed the room to embrace her friend.

"I've missed you." Faith hugged her tight and swiped at her eyes with the back of her hand. "You have to tell me all about Texas."

Gabi understood the code. Don't mention Daniel. Not at work.

It had been the same for her when her mother had been ill. Her emotions had run too close to the surface. Any questions, any well-meaning expressions of concern, could set off tears.

"Do you have time to chat for a second?" Faith motioned to the table where she'd been sitting only moments before.

"Absolutely." Gabi filled her cup with water then slipped into a chair opposite Faith.

"Now, tell me. How's your dad?"

"He's doing great."

Faith leaned forward, resting her arms on the table. "What did you think about Horseback Hill?"

"Horseback Hollow," Gabi gently corrected. "And it was great, too. A nice little town with a lot of wonderful people. Papi was so happy to have me there."

"I know you were always close." Faith reached over and covered Gabi's hand, gave it a squeeze. "Did Rosemary tell you we had an office pool on whether you'd come back? A lot of us—me included—thought you'd find a rugged cowboy and ride off into the sunset with him."

"There are definitely good-looking men in Texas." The lighthearted words were too close to the truth and emotion clogged her throat. Gabi took a sip of water to clear it. "But we both know finding the right one is hard."

A shadow slipped across Faith's face then disappeared. "I got lucky. Daniel was perfect for me."

By mentioning her husband's name, Faith had eased open the recently closed door. Gabi took a tentative step inside. "How are you doing?"

"I'm taking it a day at a time." Tears swam in Faith's eyes. "It's so surreal. I never imagined my life with him would be over so soon."

Would you do it again? Gabi wanted to ask. *Knowing what you know now, would you do it again?*

Faith gazed into her eyes and for a second it was as if her friend could read her thoughts.

"I loved Daniel. I will treasure every day we had together." Faith met Gabi's gaze. "If God had told me before we married that I could have him for only three years before he'd be called home, I'd still have walked down that aisle. I believe what a person should fear, even more than losing the one you love, is never loving at all."

When Faith left to return to her desk, Gabi remained seated. The doctors had told her she stood a good chance of living a long, healthy life, but she knew that was no guarantee. What she'd failed to consider was that no one's life came with a guarantee.

She'd been angry with Rosemary for not telling her about Daniel's death, for taking the de-

cision to return to Miami for his funeral out of
her hands. Granted, it would have been difficult to leave her father when he'd been so ill,
but she deserved to be given the information so
she could make the choice herself. She'd railed
against the injustice. Yet, hadn't she done the
same thing to Jude?

She never gave him a choice.

Gabi picked up her phone and stared at the
screen. Booking a return ticket to Horseback Hollow so soon probably didn't make sense. Unless
you were a woman with a strong, healthy heart
who was willing to put that heart on the line for
love.

She felt the warmth of the championship
ring between her breasts as the airline website
popped up and her fingers began to tap.

Chapter 18

Gabi had always enjoyed the energy of Miami International Airport. But this morning she was preoccupied as she navigated a crowded security checkpoint.

Yesterday, after her conversation with Faith, she'd booked a one-way ticket to Horseback Hollow then resigned her position at the bank. Though being without a job was a bit scary, Gabi knew, regardless of what happened between her and Jude, Miami was no longer her home.

She gave her landlord thirty days' notice and made arrangements to have professional movers pack and ship those items she wanted to keep. Rosemary and Faith had assured her they'd take care of disposing of everything else.

Once those tasks were completed, she'd called her father.

Orlando had sounded thrilled to hear she was moving to Horseback Hollow. There had been a lilt in his voice when he informed her that he and Chico would keep the light on for her. Recalling the reference to a popular motel slogan made her smile even now.

Once her feet hit Texas soil, Gabi planned to call Jude and ask him to meet her at The Grill. She'd figure out exactly what she was going to say during the five-hour flight to Lubbock. But she already knew her confession would include a heartfelt, "I'm sorry I wasn't honest with you."

She'd just been cleared through gate security when her phone dinged, announcing a text. Gabi heaved a sigh. Her father had been on a texting marathon all morning.

It was as if she was a child flying alone for the first time. He was obsessed with tracking her every movement. She didn't have to read the latest text to know what it said.

Where R U?

Gabi eased out of the line of foot traffic. Dropping her carry-on to her feet, she relaxed against a wall and texted back.

At MIA. Just cleared security.

Then, because she knew he'd ask, she added,

Heading to Field of Greens for lunch.

Chili dog, fries and large shake?

Hahaha, she texted back.

Good luck.

Gabi pulled her brows together. What kind of response was that? Did he know something about Field of Greens she didn't? Or was he simply trying to be funny?

For a second she considered asking, but immediately banished the thought. A question like that was practically guaranteed to launch a slew of additional texts.

She wanted quiet. A moment to herself. Which was a joke considering Miami International was one of the busiest airports in the country. Yet, when Gabi picked up her bag and began walking in the direction of the café known for its healthy cuisine, the mass of humanity miraculously parted in front of her.

That's when Gabi saw him. That's when her heart stopped. Just. Stopped.

Striding toward her in jeans and white T-shirt with a familiar Stetson on his head was Jude. *Her* Jude.

She increased her pace, hurrying toward him until she was almost running. When she realized she was about to plow into him, she abruptly halted. Jude covered the last few feet to her.

"Hi." With sudden awkwardness, she shifted her bag from one hand to the other. "I didn't expect to see you in Miami."

He swiped the hat off his head, raked a hand through his dark blond hair. "I'm here on business."

Her heart dropped. "Oh."

Gabi told herself she was being foolish. After the way she'd treated him, could she really believe he'd fly all this way to see her? But what kind of business could he have in Miami?

Ignoring the grumbles and muttered curses from travelers forced to scoot around them, Jude hooked his thumbs in the pockets of his jeans and rocked back on his heels.

"How about a drink?" He gestured with a jerk of his head to a nearby bar designed to look like a Mexican cantina. "Can I buy you one?"

Gabi experienced a surge of hope. At least he wasn't in a hurry to rush off. While it might be simply wishful thinking, his eyes appeared more watchful than angry.

She offered him her best smile. "I'd love a ginger ale."

He put the strap of his duffel crosswise over his body then hefted her overnight bag from her hands. On the short walk to the bar, Gabi resisted the urge to fill the silence with nervous chatter. A hostess led them to a table overlooking the runway and a server quickly took their drink order.

Jude glanced at the bag he'd placed by her chair. "Going somewhere?"

Hoping to lighten the mood, Gabi playfully brought a finger to her lips. "Airport. Suitcase. What was your first clue?"

When that adorable grin of his flashed, the tightness gripping her chest eased.

"I'm on my way back to Texas. Horseback Hollow is going to be my home," Gabi announced. "Keep your fingers crossed the position at the Vicker's Corners bank is still open."

"Last I heard" was all he said.

Her nerves, which had started to calm, began to jitter. Gabi nodded her thanks as the server returned with their drinks as well as a bowl of tortilla chips and sauce. Without thinking, she grabbed a handful of red-and-black chips and popped a couple into her mouth.

Jude lifted the bottle of Corona to his lips. "I thought you didn't eat junk food."

She dropped her gaze to the single chip left in her hand and flushed.

"Because of your heart transplant," he said pointedly then took a long pull of beer.

Gabi lowered the chip, her mouth suddenly dry as dust. She'd planned to ease into the transplant talk, dip her toe into the water before starting to swim. Now she stood teetering on the edge of the deep end where she could be over her head in seconds.

Taking a breath, she plunged in. "I owe you an apology."

He popped a couple of chips into his mouth then washed them down with another pull of beer.

"I'm sorry. *Very* sorry. I should have told you about the transplant from the beginning instead of keeping it a secret."

"Yes, you should have." Those brilliant blue eyes remained cool.

"I was convinced there could never be anything between us other than sex." She winced when his face went stony. "I was lying to myself. I was scared."

"Of what?" Confusion blanketed his face. "What were you afraid of? Be specific."

Gabi thought longingly of the flying time she'd counted on to organize her thoughts. But she didn't have the luxury of five hours in the air. Jude was sitting across from her now.

Folding her hands in her lap, Gabi cleared her throat. "When my mother was diagnosed with cancer and given a not-so-good prognosis, the knowledge that he might lose the woman he loved sliced my father in two. I saw a decorated air force officer, a man who'd flown in battle more times than I could count, break down and cry. When she passed away…"

Gabi closed her eyes for a second and willed herself to settle.

"They'd been together a long time," Jude commented.

"If you add in the time they dated, well over forty years." Gabi moistened her suddenly dry lips. "Seeing a strong man crumble had a profound impact on me. I started thinking that one in four heart transplant patients aren't alive in ten years. How could I get serious with any man, knowing what he could face?"

His gaze dragged slowly down to the tips of her hot-pink toenails in heeled sandals and back up again, lingering on the formfitting royal-blue cotton tee. "You look healthy to me."

"I've done well. My doctors call me their star patient." For the first time since she'd begun her explanation, Gabi smiled. "Not a single rejection episode. I let myself be encouraged by the fact I'd stayed healthy. But recently—"

At her hesitation, concern flashed across Jude's face like a bolt of lightning.

"Nothing with me," she quickly assured him. "But Mary, a woman who'd had a transplant around the same time as me, passed away before Christmas. She'd had some issues over the years, but none I saw as life-threatening. Then shortly before I came to Horseback Hollow, Kate—another fellow transplant recipient—called me, distraught. Although she had no symptoms, her annual cardiac biopsy showed evidence of rejection."

Out of the corner of her eye Gabi saw the waitress approach the table. Jude waved her off.

"Despite my reservations, I convinced myself we could make it work." Gabi closed her eyes for a second, breathed out. "Then I went to the luncheon at your mom's house."

"Piper" was all he said.

"Yes." Despite Gabi's efforts to control it, her voice turned wistful. "When I held her, when I saw the look on your face, I knew, *I knew,* you were picturing me with our child."

The look in his eyes told her she'd gotten it right.

"My cardiologist has discouraged me from getting pregnant. How could I possibly consider a future with you, knowing I couldn't give you a son or daughter of your own?"

"When you told me our relationship was only about sex, you spoke the truth." His voice was heavy with resignation.

"No." She expelled a shaky breath, gave a little laugh. "I broke my own rule. I fell in love with you."

With trembling fingers, Gabi lifted the ring hanging from a slender gold chain out from beneath her shirt. "I should have left this behind. I couldn't. In my mind, as long as I had it, the connection to you stayed intact. Even though we were apart, it was as if you were still with me."

Jude didn't say a word but she nearly wept when he reached across the small table and took her hand.

"I don't understand," he said slowly. "Why are you willing to consider a future with me now when you were so opposed before? What changed?"

"I realize life comes with no guarantees." Gabi quickly told him about her conversation with Faith. "I love you, Jude, and I really can't do without you. Just so we're clear, it was never just about the sex. Although I have to admit that was pretty spectacular."

His grin flashed.

"I just want to make sure you understand.

Though my cardiologist may reconsider his stance, there's a very real possibility I might not be able to have a child." Gabi met his gaze. "I realize how important family is to you. You want children."

She said it as fact, instead of a question, knowing she spoke the truth. And if he denied it, he'd be not only lying to her but to himself.

"Of course I want kids. So do you."

Gabi slowly nodded.

"You don't have to give birth to them." His voice softened and he squeezed the hand he still held. "There are so many options nowadays. We could adopt, either a baby or an older child. We could use a surrogate. And if, when it's all said and done, it ends up just being the two of us, I'd be okay with that, too. What I'm not okay with is being without you."

Her heart hitched. Still, she refused to minimize what he might face in the future. "While I've done well since my transplant, something could go wrong without warning."

"Darlin'," he drawled, in a thick Texas accent that made blood slide like warm honey through her veins. "A horse could toss me tomorrow and I could break my neck. There are no guarantees for any of us."

"That's true. But just so you understand—"

"What I understand, what I insist on, is no more lies between us."

She swallowed hard, gave a jerky nod.

"One more thing." He paused. "I'd like my ring back."

Pain rose inside Gabi with a force so strong tears spurted to her eyes. Fumbling badly, she managed to pull the chain over her head then handed it to him with fingers that trembled.

With a careless gesture, he dropped the ring and chain to the table.

She'd given him the information. He'd made the decision to break their connection. The ground that had seemed so firm only seconds earlier was disintegrating beneath her feet. Jude clasped her hand in his for what she assumed was a final goodbye.

His choice, she reminded herself, blinking back tears.

"I remember the first time I saw you. It was like being kicked by a mule. I dated a lot of women in the past but never wanted to stick with any of them. Now I know why. I was waiting for you." His lips curved. "But I see now that starting off as friends gave our relationship a rock-solid foundation."

For a second his gaze dropped to the championship ring and chain lying on the table. Then he lifted his gaze and those eyes, clear and so very blue, pinned her. "Going steady was good. But not enough. Not nearly enough."

As she struggled to remember how to breathe, he continued, his voice deep and thick with emotion.

"I want more. I need more." Jude spread his hands in a helpless gesture. "I love you, Gabi. I can't imagine my life without you in it. Whether God gives us fifty days or fifty years, I want to spend them all with you."

Before she could comprehend what was happening, Jude dropped down on one knee and snapped open a small velvet box. A sparkling square-cut diamond flashed fire while love blazed strong in his eyes. "Gabriella Mendoza, will you do me the honor of becoming my wife?"

Tears streamed down Gabi's cheeks. Now that it was her time to speak, all she could do was nod. Oh, and hold out her hand for him to slide that gorgeous ring on her finger.

The bar, which had quieted during the proposal, erupted into cheers and applause.

"Way to go, cowboy," someone yelled.

Jude rose, tugged her up against him. "We're going to be so happy."

"Guaranteed," Gabi murmured as his lips closed over hers.

* * * * *

Get 4 FREE REWARDS!

We'll send you 2 FREE Books plus <u>2</u> FREE Mystery Gifts.

Harlequin® Special Edition books feature heroines finding the balance between their work life and personal life on the way to finding true love.

FREE
Value Over
$20

Get 4 FREE REWARDS!

We'll send you 2 FREE Books plus 2 FREE Mystery Gifts.

Harlequin® Romance Larger-Print books feature uplifting escapes that will warm your heart with the ultimate feel-good tales.

FREE
Value Over
$20

YES! Please send me 2 FREE Harlequin® Romance Larger-Print novels and my 2 FREE gifts (gifts are worth about $10 retail). After receiving them, if I don't wish to receive any more books, I can return the shipping statement marked "cancel." If I don't cancel, I will receive 4 brand-new novels every month and be billed just $5.34 per book in the U.S. or $5.74 per book in Canada. That's a savings of at least 15% off the cover price! It's quite a bargain! Shipping and handling is just 50¢ per book in the U.S. and 75¢ per book in Canada.* I understand that accepting the 2 free books and gifts places me under no obligation to buy anything. I can always return a shipment and cancel at any time. The free books and gifts are mine to keep no matter what I decide.

119/319 HDN GMYY

Name (please print)

Address   Apt. #

City   State/Province   Zip/Postal Code

Mail to the **Reader Service:**
IN U.S.A.: P.O. Box 1341, Buffalo, NY 14240-8531
IN CANADA: P.O. Box 603, Fort Erie, Ontario L2A 5X3

Want to try 2 free books from another series? Call 1-800-873-8635 or visit www.ReaderService.com.

Get 4 FREE REWARDS!

We'll send you 2 FREE Books plus 2 FREE Mystery Gifts.

FREE Value Over **$20**

Both the **Romance** and **Suspense** collections feature compelling novels written by many of today's best-selling authors.

YES! Please send me 2 FREE novels from the Essential Romance or Essential Suspense Collection and my 2 FREE gifts (gifts are worth about $10 retail). After receiving them, if I don't wish to receive any more books, I can return the shipping statement marked "cancel." If I don't cancel, I will receive 4 brand-new novels every month and be billed just $6.74 each in the U.S. or $7.24 each in Canada. That's a savings of at least 16% off the cover price. It's quite a bargain! Shipping and handling is just 50¢ per book in the U.S. and 75¢ per book in Canada.* I understand that accepting the 2 free books and gifts places me under no obligation to buy anything. I can always return a shipment and cancel at any time. The free books and gifts are mine to keep no matter what I decide.

Choose one: ☐ **Essential Romance**   ☐ **Essential Suspense**
              (194/394 MDN GMY7)   (191/391 MDN GMY7)

Name (please print)

Address   Apt. #

City   State/Province   Zip/Postal Code

Mail to the **Reader Service:**
IN U.S.A.: P.O. Box 1341, Buffalo, NY 14240-8531
IN CANADA: P.O. Box 603, Fort Erie, Ontario L2A 5X3

Want to try 2 free books from another series? Call 1-800-873-8635 or visit www.ReaderService.com.

Get 4 FREE REWARDS!

We'll send you 2 FREE Books plus 2 FREE Mystery Gifts.

Harlequin® Heartwarming™ Larger-Print books feature traditional values of home, family, community and—most of all—love.

FREE
Value Over
$20

YES! Please send me 2 FREE Harlequin® Heartwarming™ Larger-Print novels and my 2 FREE mystery gifts (gifts worth about $10 retail). After receiving them, if I don't wish to receive any more books, I can return the shipping statement marked "cancel." If I don't cancel, I will receive 4 brand-new larger-print novels every month and be billed just $5.49 per book in the U.S. or $6.24 per book in Canada. That's a savings of at least 19% off the cover price. It's quite a bargain! Shipping and handling is just 50¢ per book in the U.S. and 75¢ per book in Canada.* I understand that accepting the 2 free books and gifts places me under no obligation to buy anything. I can always return a shipment and cancel at any time. The free books and gifts are mine to keep no matter what I decide.

161/361 IDN GMY3

Name (please print)

Address   Apt. #

City   State/Province   Zip/Postal Code

Mail to the Reader Service:
IN U.S.A.: P.O. Box 1341, Buffalo, NY 14240-8531
IN CANADA: P.O. Box 603, Fort Erie, Ontario L2A 5X3

Want to try 2 free books from another series! Call 1-800-873-8635 or visit www.ReaderService.com.